Cassie at the Ballet School

As the three girls neared the sleeping school, they grew quieter.

'I just hope Miss Wrench is out of the way now,' whispered Emily.

'Of course she will be,' said Cassie. She sounded more confident than she felt.

Their heavy outdoor shoes clanged on the fire-escape as they went up. Cassie pushed against the door – nothing happened!

'It's jammed!' she hissed.

They all put their shoulders to the door, but it stayed firmly shut.

Becky groaned. 'What are we going to do? All the doors will be locked by this time.'

Cassie was staring at the window next to the fire-escape.

'Look!' she said. 'They've left it open. I can climb on to the window-ledge!'

'No!' cried Emily, 'you might fall!'

But Cassie was already steeling herself for the climb . . .

The Ballet School series

Cassie at the Ballet School

Mal Lewis Jones

Hodder
Children's
Books

a division of Hodder Headline plc

Special thanks to Freed of London Ltd., 94 St Martins Lane,
London WC2N for the loan of dance wear

Children for cover illustration courtesy of Gaston Payne School
of Theatre, Dance and Drama

Copyright © Mal Lewis Jones 1994

The right of Mal Lewis Jones to be identified as the Author of
the Work has been asserted by her in accordance with the
Copyright, Designs and Patents Act 1988.

First published in Great Britain by Hodder Children's Books in 1994

10 9 8 7 6 5 4 3 2

All rights reserved. No part of this publication may be
reproduced, stored in a retrieval system, or transmitted,
in any form or by any means without the prior written
permission of the publisher, nor be otherwise circulated
in any form of binding or cover other than that in which
it is published and without a similar condition being
imposed on the subsequent purchaser.

All characters in this publication are fictitious
and any resemblance to real persons, living or dead,
is purely coincidental.

A catalogue record for this title is available from the British Library

ISBN 0 340 60729 7

Typeset by Avon Dataset Ltd, Bidford-on-Avon

Printed and bound in Great Britain by
Cox & Wyman Ltd, Reading, Berks.

Hodder Children's Books
A Division of Hodder Headline plc
338 Euston Road
London NW1 3BH

Contents

For Claire Johnson

1

An Unexpected Meeting

Long before the rising bell at seven, Cassie Brown opened her eyes and was instantly wide awake. She felt excited and nervous, in an equal mixture. How strange to be waking up in a room miles away from her own familiar bedroom at home! And even stranger to be sharing it with two girls she hardly knew!

Her own bed was the middle one. In the watery September sunshine filtering through the floral curtains, she glanced at the sleeping heads either side of her – one dark, one fair. Cassie hadn't really taken to the dark-haired girl, Amanda Renwick.

But her other room-mate, Becky Hastings, the one with blonde, almost white hair, she had liked from the start. Cassie had met them both for the first time the previous afternoon, Sunday – the day they had all arrived with their parents and luggage at Redwood Ballet School.

Cassie wondered if she dare get out of bed. Would it wake the other two? She couldn't wait to get dressed in the new, crisp, grey and red uniform hanging in the wardrobe, ready for her first day. There had been no uniform at the little village primary school she used to attend.

She sighed. The longing to get up was becoming unbearable, like an itch you just have to scratch. She carefully peeled off her bedcovers and crawled to the end of the bed, where her reflection in the large wardrobe mirror made her jump! She smiled into the glass, and then frowned as she noticed, as she always did, how her front teeth stuck out a bit. The gap between them seemed to have grown even larger. How she wished her eyes were violet, not brown, and her hair a more dramatic colour, like jet black or flaming red!

Even my name is Brown! she thought to herself. *Still, I suppose the rest of me isn't too bad.*

As she crept past Becky's bed, there was suddenly a snorting noise and then a pink and white face appeared from under the quilt.

'Morning, early bird!' Becky said, cheerfully.

'Shh!' warned Cassie. 'Amanda's still asleep.'

At that moment, Amanda groaned and turned over, but she didn't wake up.

'I was just going to have a bath,' whispered Cassie.

Becky pulled a face. 'Oh, don't bother. It's such a waste of time. You only get dirty again.' She grinned. 'Stay and chat to me instead.'

'OK,' Cassie said and curled up on Becky's bed. 'I can't wait to get started.'

'Nor can I. What time's breakfast?'

'Seven-thirty I think. Another hour yet.'

Becky opened her bedside drawer, took out a packet of chocolate biscuits and offered one to Cassie.

'Thanks, I'm starving,' said Cassie gratefully.

'That'll keep you going till breakfast. Let's hope it's a bit better than supper last night. Yuck!'

Cassie thought of the over-crisp fried fish and the soggy chips. 'Couldn't be much worse!'

'Don't worry,' said Becky, grinning. 'If you're ever hungry, let me know. Mum's left me *loads* of goodies.' She licked her lips and rolled her eyes.

'What was that?' Amanda sat up and stretched gracefully. 'Did somebody mention food?'

'Just talking about how awful supper was last night,' Becky said.

'Yes, it was a bit of a come-down,' said Amanda.

Becky gave her a biscuit and Amanda nibbled at it elegantly. She seemed very sophisticated.

The day before, her father and another man had brought up lots of expensive suitcases full of fashionable clothes. But what put Cassie most in awe of her was her bored expression and her beautifully modelled head – a dancer's head, with olive skin, high cheekbones and a long, graceful neck.

Becky rolled back her quilt and yawned, and suddenly Cassie couldn't sit still any longer.

'Come on! Race you to the bathroom!' she said, grabbing her towel. Becky scrambled out of bed behind her and they dashed across the landing to the bathroom, falling over each other to be first in. Cassie won.

'First the worst, second the best!' gasped Becky. She ran over to the window. 'Let's have a look outside.'

'What can you see?' asked Cassie, craning round her.

'Fruit trees! We'll be able to go fruit-picking in a few weeks' time if we're lucky. Just like at home!'

She pointed out the orchard far away, at the edge of the grounds.

'Hey, look at that!' Cassie peered out of the window. 'I didn't notice that yesterday. There's a ruin or something behind the trees.'

'Yes, you're right,' said Becky, 'and it looks as though it's this side of the boundary wall. I wonder what it is?'

'We must find out. Oh, I *love* ruins. They're so exciting!'

The bathroom door swung open and a small girl

4

walked in, puffy-eyed from crying. Cassie stared at her in amazement.

'Emily!' she exclaimed, and ran over to grab her hands.

Emily was startled at first, but when she realised who Cassie was, a huge smile transformed her face.

'I can't believe you're here!' said Cassie. 'I didn't see you last night. I didn't think you'd made it!'

'Oh, Mum couldn't bring me till late. She works on Sundays. I got here just in time for bed,' Emily said.

Cassie introduced Emily to Becky.

'Which room are you in?' she asked.

Emily pointed to the door next to theirs.

'Oh that's great!' cried Cassie. 'Next-door neighbours. We'll be able to visit each other late at night.'

'Not after lights out, you won't,' said a second year, who had just come into the bathroom.

'No one'll know,' said Cassie.

'House-mothers have super-hearing,' said the girl.

'Our house-mother seems really nice,' Cassie retorted.

The second year laughed. 'Miss Eiseldown still has to keep to the rules. And there are plenty of those at Redwood.'

Cassie shrugged and turned back to Emily. She felt truly amazed to be meeting her again.

'I can't believe it!' she kept repeating, until Becky tried to sit on her to shut her up.

'Go and jump in your bath,' said Becky. 'It might *dampen* you down!'

Scrubbing vigorously in the hot water a few minutes later, Cassie thought back to the nerve-wracking weekend last February when she had first met Emily.

It had been Cassie's first sight of the ballet school, an imposing red brick mansion house at the end of a long curving gravel drive. There were shaved lawns either side of the drive, fringed along the edges with the gigantic redwood trees from which the school took its name.

Redwood. Cassie's romantic visions had not been disappointed. In the spacious entrance hall, the first thing she noticed was an enormous full-length portrait of a beautiful dancer in a Giselle costume. On the same wall were dozens of framed photographs of dancers and teachers who had connections with the school.

The hall had an impressive stone fireplace with a carved crest above it, and a sweeping staircase at the far end. The walls were wood-panelled and the floor, too, was polished wood of a golden-brown colour. From the centre of the ceiling, which itself was decorated with plaster flowers and leaves, hung a magnificent chandelier.

But despite the size of the room, it soon became difficult to move: the hall was choked with children and parents, all here for the final audition at the ballet school – an audition which would last two whole days.

Cassie ducked her head back under the blistering hot water, sat up and wrung out her shoulder-length hair. Two days! It had felt like two *weeks!*

Out of something like 4,000 applicants, Cassie was one of the final few hundred to get through the regional rounds and be called for this second audition. The hopeful young dancers were competing for about thirty places – twenty for the girls, ten for the boys.

After changing into their ballet kit, they were divided into groups by a business-like young woman in a dark grey suit, with a clipboard under her arm. Cassie's group was ushered into Studio One and she marvelled at the lovely room, the mirrors and the fixed barres at two different heights, running along two walls.

There was an excited buzz as the girls chatted nervously to one another. This was when Cassie met Emily. Nearly a head shorter than Cassie, with fair-brown hair, blue eyes and very pale skin, Emily seemed to know what was going on, which was a comfort to Cassie who hadn't a clue. For instance, she whispered to Cassie that the teacher with the clipboard was called Miss Oakland.

A hush fell as another teacher entered the studio. The girls waited with quiet anticipation for their first command. Unexpectedly, it was something very simple, just skipping around the room to some lively music. Cassie felt the tension ebbing from her muscles and the old joy of moving.

Exercises at the barre were gone through with great concentration, but again, they were fairly basic exercises which everybody would know. Then they were asked to leave the barre and begin their centre work. Cassie noticed for the first time that the woman with the clipboard was watching them and that she was taking notes. This made her feel nervous again, and she was glad when they were asked to do a free movement sequence which consisted of jumping from an arabesque with foot extended behind, to an attitude with the front leg, changing feet with a neat pattern of steps. She threw herself into this sequence and again managed to forget anyone was watching her.

After that, there was a short break for a drink and a biscuit. Children swarmed back to their mums and dads in the dining hall, chattering nineteen to the dozen, everyone eager and full of hope.

Then, shock waves. The grey-suited woman reappeared: a messenger. She had a list on her clipboard of names which she read aloud.

'Joanne Smith, Zoe Barnes, Alison Goodwin, Maria Crespi, Pippa Johnson, Catherine Wood, Amita Gupta, Laura Hughes. Thank you. You won't be needed any longer.'

There was a moment's stunned silence. Then a girl broke out in hysterical crying.

Cassie felt shaken. She could hardly believe that the teachers had made up their minds that they didn't want those poor girls already. And after all they must have been through to get this far!

'Are you sure my name wasn't on the list, Mum?'

'Yes, Cassie, quite sure.'

Her mum and dad exchanged horrified glances. None of them had expected such brusque treatment. Joy Brown looked over sympathetically at the hysterical girl, who was being comforted by her mother.

But Cassie had no more time to worry about it – she was called to another class, and again found herself next to Emily. This took place in Studio Two, which was a carbon copy of Studio One, but with everything the other way round.

'That was horrible, wasn't it?' said Emily. 'After coming all this way, and only doing one class.'

'Yes,' agreed Cassie, 'then being told to go away, just like that. I hope the same thing doesn't happen again before the end of the audition.'

But after the last class of the day, which was taken by a French teacher, and when Cassie and Emily were eating tea with Cassie's parents and Emily's mum, the dreaded woman with the clipboard reappeared.

The noisy clattery tea-time sounds died down. The grey-suited woman didn't have to raise her voice.

'Charles Wood, Timothy Banks, Roy Fulwood . . .'

9

'Boys' names,' thought Cassie. 'Oh, please, please, *please* don't let there be any girls on this list!'

'John Smithson, Pieter Schmidt, William Robinson,' continued the woman. 'Thank you for attending. You won't be required any longer.'

Cassie let out a sigh of relief. Her eye caught Emily's. They smiled at one another.

But for the not-so-lucky ones, it was all over. Several families were gathering their belongings together hurriedly, some of them angrily.

One boy passed their table, and Cassie heard his father say, 'This is all your fault! It's all been for nothing. What a waste of time and effort!' As the man went out of the door, he banged it behind him loudly.

'Well, he didn't seem too pleased,' said Jake Brown, as light-heartedly as he could.

'He nearly took the door off its hinges!' added Cassie's mum.

The girls both giggled but Cassie noticed that Emily's mum remained unsmiling. She seemed to frown all the time.

By lunch-time on the second day, Cassie's name had still not been called, and nor had Emily's, but hopes were no longer so buoyant. There was tension in the air.

Cassie was given a full orthopaedic examination by the school's visiting consultant, followed by X-rays of hands, spine and feet. She was measured and weighed and her mother and father had to give her full medical history. The attendant explained that the hand and foot X-rays were to give some indication of how much more growing she would do. Already taller than average, this made Cassie anxious. They didn't want dancers who would look taller on pointe than their male partners. On the other hand, they didn't want girls who would be obviously smaller than the rest of the corps de ballet.

'Wouldn't it be awful,' she whispered to her mum, 'if they thought my dancing was good enough, but the X-rays showed I'd be too tall.'

'Well, better to know at this stage than when you've spent years and years training to be a dancer,' said Joy.

On being asked to show her best 'frogs' legs', Cassie obediently sat down, splaying her knees outwards till they rested comfortably on the floor. The teacher smiled.

'No trouble to you, is it?' She spoke with a French accent. Cassie smiled back. It was the first trace of warmth she had encountered since the audition began.

The nice teacher asked her to stand at the barre, where she manipulated first Cassie's left leg, then her right, to ascertain the amount of flexibility in her hip joints.

'Merci,' she said. 'Very good. Now number twenty-one.'

Number twenty-one was, in fact, Emily. She grinned at Cassie as they changed places. Cassie thought how pretty she was when she smiled; most of the time she looked pale and anxious.

Praise was very sparse during these two days. It was rather like trying to please gods who were seldom impressed by anything.

Her parents were interviewed by the principal, Miss Wrench, and three of the staff, while Cassie was being put through her paces in yet another ballet class. They came out looking almost as exhausted as she did.

'Phew!' said her father. 'That was worse than my last job interview!'

'Never mind, Dad!' chipped in Cassie. 'You'll think it was worth it when I'm a famous ballerina.'

But in spite of her tiredness, by the end of the weekend, Cassie was still high with excitement. She spent the last few minutes chatting to Emily; at the back of her mind was the thought that they might never meet again.

'Hurry up, Emily,' snapped her mother. Cassie thought how thin and harassed she looked. 'I must get home to the others.'

Emily quickly said goodbye and followed her mum, who was already halfway across the foyer.

'Do you think I'll get in, Mum?' asked Cassie as she bounced into the Browns' car. Joy turned and looked at her. Her daughter's face was flushed, her eyes sparkled and that chin looked as obstinate as ever.

'Time will tell,' said Joy, with a sigh. 'Time will tell.'

2

Wrong-Footed

Cassie's stomach jolted as Miss Oakland rapped sharply on the wooden piano. The class of first years stopped the sequence they were dancing abruptly.

'No, no!' she said. 'COUNT ONE. Sissonne ouverte with the *right* foot. COUNT TWO. Coupé under with the *right* foot and assemble under with the *left* foot.'

Miss Oakland, though young, smart and attractive, was a hard task-master and hadn't a great deal of patience. She nodded to the pianist and the class began again, for the third time. She stood over them all, her beginners, like a kestrel watching a family of mice.

Cassie was watching her own reflection in the floor-to-ceiling mirrors on the opposite wall. She was the tallest in the class and looked slender as a young willow in her new baby-pink leotard. For a moment, her concentration lapsed.

Clapping for them to stop again, Miss Oakland moved over briskly to Cassie.

'Cassandra!' she exclaimed. 'Do you know your left foot from your right? Would you like me to stick labels on them for you?'

The class tittered at her sarcastic tone. Cassie noticed a sneering sort of smile on Amanda's face and felt hot with embarrassment and anger. She turned bright red. She had been warned that life at Redwood Ballet School wouldn't be easy, but that had never stopped her from trying to get there. And now it was her very first ballet class and she was finding out for herself just how hard it was.

As the music restarted, Cassie's body automatically repeated the exercise. It was all so different from the ballet classes she used to attend at her local dancing school in the church hall. No mirror-lined studio then. No fitted barres and smooth, golden wood floors. Just a large, draughty hall and rickety old chairs to hold on to for barre work. Her teacher, Miss Lakeley, had made it quite clear to everyone that Cassie was her most promising pupil. Cassie could picture her now – a plump, friendly woman, who always wore a headscarf and large looped earrings. She called them all her chicks and was always encouraging, even to the girls who were absolutely hopeless at dancing.

How different from Miss Oakland, thought Cassie, as she finished the sequence and found, to her consternation, that she had yet again landed on the wrong foot. She looked up quickly, hoping against hope that Miss Oakland hadn't noticed. But the teacher was glaring at her, hands on hips.

'Cassandra. You must *concentrate!* You'll find slipshod work will not be tolerated here.'

Cassie felt as though she were burning up. She felt the eyes of all the other girls – most of them strangers – upon her. Why had she so longed to come here, she asked herself miserably. The other girls were all so good, so *very* good. She was so used to being the best in the class, without even having to try all that hard. But here, the standard was much higher, the pace much tougher.

She felt dreadfully embarrassed when Miss Oakland went through the exercise slowly with her, on her own. Was she going to be the slowest in the class, the one who always got things wrong?

'Now perhaps everyone will at least get the correct feet,' said the teacher, raising her eyebrows at Cassie. 'But you all look half-asleep. Sissonnes should be crisp. CRISP!' she repeated more loudly, making Cassie flinch. 'I think I'd like to see you one by one.'

As Cassie walked to the back corner of the studio, she felt a squeeze on her arm. It was Emily.

'Don't take any notice,' she whispered.

Cassie was very glad of a few minutes' rest in the corner. How could she ever have thought she'd be good enough?

But after all, Miss Lakeley had believed in her. She thought back to the conversation Miss Lakeley had had with her mother about a year before, after ballet class one Saturday.

'I've been thinking about Cassandra for some time,' Miss Lakeley said . . .

'Have you?' Joy Brown asked, surprised.

'She's good. There's no denying it. And I've been wondering what's the best course.'

'Course?'

'Towards a dancing career.'

Cassie's heart gave a bound.

'I really don't think we've made up our minds that that's what Cassie's heading towards. My husband—'

'Cassandra's very *talented*, Mrs Brown,' Miss Lakeley interrupted impatiently. 'A terrible waste not to make the best of her gifts!'

'Well, I suppose so. What had you in mind?'

'First step, ballet class four times a week. Five would be better still.'

'*Five?*'

18

Cassie thought her mum was going to faint on the spot.

'No. Probably four would be fine. Because I can trust her to practise hard in between.' Miss Lakeley smiled at Cassie. 'Of course, some of the extra lessons would be on her own, so the rate would be higher.'

'But she's doing so well anyway. Is there really any need—'

'Oh yes! Definitely there is a need. If she's to stand a chance.'

'A chance of what precisely, Miss Lakeley?'

'Of an audition for Redwood Ballet School!'

Joy stood speechless. Cassie felt as if she were getting lighter and lighter. Soon she would float right up to the ceiling . . . Redwood was the top ballet school in the country, the only one funded by the government. Cassie had always longed to go there, but had never dared hope she would be good enough to try.

At last her mum managed to speak. 'I . . . I'll have to talk to Jake about this. It needs very serious thought.'

'Let me know as soon as possible,' said Miss Lakeley. 'Cassandra could begin extra classes next week. The sooner, the better.'

It was that conversation which started Cassie planning, scheming and working her hardest to get at least as far as an audition for Redwood.

The first obstacle was her parents. There were

several arguments, but Cassie was determined to win. Her mum had always said she had an obstinate chin. Now that mulish streak came to the fore.

'You *are* only ten, Cassie,' Jake Brown argued. 'It's very young to be going hammer and tongs at something you'll probably change your mind about in two or three years' time!'

'I won't change my mind!' Cassie insisted, her chin jutting out even further than usual.

'Give it another year,' said her mother. 'Time to mature a bit and see if you really do want to pursue this dancing idea.'

'But it'll be too *late* then!' cried Cassie in frustration. 'I *must* be ready for the regional auditions in October or there'll be *no* chance of getting into Redwood. And it's simply the best!'

Joy and Jake looked at one another and sighed, and Cassie knew she had won – the first stage of the battle at least.

'Ouch!'

Becky was elbowing her in the ribs.

'You're next!' she hissed, with a grin.

Cassie jumped to her feet and moved into the centre of the studio to perform the sissonne double sequence, under Miss Oakland's scrutiny. The words, *Cassandra's very talented!* flashed across her mind, like a lifebelt thrown to a swimmer in a rough sea. All her concentration centred on what she was doing and she made no mistakes this time. But after she had finished, Miss Oakland gave no hint of praise.

By the end of class, Cassie couldn't help feeling deflated but was determined not to let it show. She followed Emily and Becky into the changing room, wondering if they were feeling the same way.

'That was unbelievable!' Cassie exclaimed. 'I shall ache in parts of my body that I didn't even know I had!'

'Yes, by supper-time, we'll all be crawling round on our hands and knees,' said Becky.

Cassie laughed. Becky hadn't found it easy either.

'She's a bit of a stickler, Miss Oakland, isn't she?' remarked Emily. 'But she's supposed to be a really good teacher.'

Cassie shrugged. She still felt quite angry underneath. 'I'd like to put a label on *her*! One saying "Patience is a virtue".'

'True, she hasn't got a lot of it,' said Becky. 'I wonder what time break is?'

Emily consulted her timetable. 'It's now. Then double Geography and Junior Assembly, before lunch.'

Cassie groaned. 'Double Geography. Yuck!' It had been easy to forget, in the months of anticipation, that there would be ordinary lessons at Redwood as well as dancing.

'It's not fair!' snorted Becky. 'We'll spend most of our break getting out of our ballet things and into our grotty uniform.'

Becky looked so hard-done-by that Cassie burst out laughing. 'Get a move on then, Becky. Let's see if we can be first in the bun queue.'

But Becky didn't reply. She was already racing through the showers.

Cassie threw on her grey kilt, white blouse and red cardigan. At the back of her mind nagged the voice of her housemother. Miss Eiseldown had impressed upon them only that morning how important their appearance was. Any untidiness in uniform, either ballet or academic, would be punished with a black mark.

'Come on you two,' urged Becky, who was ready first. 'I'm dying of starvation. Two hours of ballet class is a bit much on a bowl of cornflakes and a piece of toast.'

Break proved hectic and very rushed. All too soon, they were sitting in their first school lesson. Cassie was beginning to feel rather tired and found it hard to concentrate. After Geography, they were ushered, along with the other first and second years, into the assembly hall, to meet their Principal, Miss Wrench. They were not allowed to talk, as they filed into position and then stood waiting.

Miss Wrench entered from her study and mounted the platform. She must have been in her fifties, but was still slim and erect, though old-fashioned in dress. Her hair was steely-grey and pulled back tightly into a French pleat. She wore black lace-up shoes, a pleated black skirt and a crisp white blouse. Everything about her seemed to say, 'I stand no nonsense'.

'Good morning, Juniors,' were the words she *actually* used.

'Good morning, Miss Wrench,' chorused the girls and boys in the hall.

After hymns and prayers, Miss Wrench gave the Juniors a list of DO'S and DON'TS to supplement the ones they had already learned from Miss Eiseldown, their housemother.

'And when you meet me or any of my ballet staff anywhere in the building, even if you are just passing by in the corridor, girls are expected to curtsey, and boys to bow.

'Finally,' said Miss Wrench, 'you are forbidden to go into the grounds after supper. Of course, in your free time earlier in the day, the grounds are there for you to enjoy.'

Cassie and Becky exchanged meaningful glances, each with a different thought – Cassie's of the ruin, Becky's of fruit-picking.

'Now, first years remain in the hall. You will be weighed and measured by Matron, before you go to the dining hall. Second years are dismissed.'

Miss Eiseldown took Cassie, Becky, Amanda, Emily and her room mates to Matron's, joking with them while they queued outside. She had been far more serious first thing that morning, when she had told them how to keep their beds and room in good order, and shown them a chart on the landing where gold stars would be displayed for the tidiest rooms each week.

She was one of the youngest teachers in the school, and certainly the prettiest. She had neither Miss Oakland's sharp tongue nor Miss Wrench's forbidding appearance. Cassie was pleased she was their housemother. She was also teaching them Maths.

'What's the difference between a rhinoceros, a lemon and a tube of glue?' asked Miss Eiseldown, her eyes twinkling.

'We give up! Don't know!' cried several voices together.

'Well, you can squeeze a lemon, but you can't squeeze a rhinoceros!'

'What about the tube of glue?' asked Cassie.

'I thought you might get *stuck* on that!' said Miss Eiseldown, and everybody groaned.

After the visit to Matron, the girls had their lunch. There was a proper cooked lunch, but there were plenty of salads too. Cassie's tiredness went off as soon as she walked into the dining hall, which was alive with the sounds of boys and girls laughing, talking and eating.

'Isn't it great to be here?' she said, doing a little twirl with her lunch-tray. She suddenly felt on top on the world.

'Watch it,' urged Emily. 'Miss Oakland's looking at you.'

Cassie hurriedly plonked herself down at the first

free table and was joined by Emily. Becky lingered, casting her eyes over the choice of puddings, before joining them. Emily and Cassie ran through the timetable for the rest of the day.

'Lessons again from two till four. Maths, English and double Science. Homework from four till five. Character class from five till six-thirty. Supper six thirty. Bedtime eight thirty.'

Becky almost choked on her pizza. 'You mean we don't get anything to eat from now till six thirty!' She quickly left the table to try and get seconds of the apple pie.

Cassie went quiet. She was beginning to feel apprehensive about her next dance class. Would she keep up with everyone else? She'd thought the worst bit was over, once she'd got through that terrible audition.

'Penny for them!' said Emily.

'What?'

'Your thoughts.'

'I was just thinking about our audition,' said Cassie.

'Mmm,' said Emily. 'It was nice that we met there, and we both got in. A lot of people didn't, did they?'

'No,' said Cassie. 'We were amazingly lucky.'

'The way I felt last night, I wasn't so sure.'

'Were you homesick?'

'I just missed my mum,' said Emily. 'But I'm feeling heaps better today.'

She leaned forward across the table. 'Do you

know that at the end of the first year, they chuck out about ten students?'

Cassie looked at her in horror. 'Oh, that's awful, Emily! I didn't know that.' She wondered what her own chances were of staying at Redwood for longer than twelve months.

'Do you think it'll be Miss Oakland taking us for our Character class?'

'No, don't worry,' replied Emily with a smile. 'It's a teacher called Mrs Bonsing.'

'I hope she's less sarcastic,' said Cassie, nervously.

But her fears were needless. When five o'clock came round, after their afternoon school and homework, Mrs Bonsing welcomed the girls into the studio with a beaming smile. She was round and jolly-looking, with short frizzy hair and bright red lipstick. Cassie couldn't help staring at her legs, which were knobbly with protruding veins. But once Mrs Bonsing started demonstrating a polka step to them, her rather grotesque appearance was forgotten. She was so nimble and light on her feet!

Cassie stopped worrying and let herself relax. It was lovely to dance confidently, in the midst of a group of dancers, all swirling their pretty ribbon-strewn skirts and clicking the heels of their black Character shoes. Halfway through the lesson, Mrs Bonsing asked Becky to demonstrate a sequence to the others, which she did so rhythmically that Cassie saw for the first time how her friend had managed to get into Redwood.

At seven o'clock, their supper over, the girls returned to their own rooms. Cassie didn't know if she'd be able to wait until eight thirty for bedtime – she was so tired! But Becky still seemed full of energy and popped next door to see Emily.

Amanda was lying full-length on her bed. She stretched and sat up.

'I think I'll do a spot of practice before lights out,' she said.

'I'm too shattered tonight,' said Cassie. 'Isn't it a bit late at night for practice?'

'Oh no,' said Amanda. 'They encourage you to use the private practice rooms after supper.'

Amanda still wore the regulation red tracksuit over her leotard, so she only had to take her ballet shoes along with her.

Why do people like Amanda always look fantastic, whatever they're wearing? wondered Cassie.

Becky poked her head round the door – a strong contrast to the sleek Amanda, her plaits half undone, with tufts of hair sticking out all over the place.

'Wow! You look very glamorous, I must say!' laughed Cassie.

'Come and join us!' Becky said, grinning. 'And bring your pillow.'

Full of curiosity, Cassie followed Becky into the corridor, where she could hear shrieks and thuds coming from next door. Five second years from further down the landing had invaded Emily's room and started a pillow-fight.

It was a much bigger room than Cassie's – a dormitory really, with seven beds. Cassie launched herself into the fray, her tiredness forgotten as she biffed one of the second years from behind with her pillow. The girl squared up to her new opponent and a ferocious duel continued till they both collapsed in hysterical giggles.

In the corner, Becky and several other girls were standing on the beds pummelling each other. Bedclothes and ornaments were all over the floor. As the fight became frenetic, Cassie was dimly aware, between fits of laughter, of footsteps crossing the floor above their heads. Suddenly, the second year who had been her opponent jumped up, grabbed her friends and scuttled out of the room with them.

Cassie realised something was wrong, but before she had a chance to warn the others there was a loud knock on the door. Without waiting for an answer, Miss Eiseldown strode in, looking very cross.

'What on earth have you been doing?' she demanded.

As this question hardly needed answering, the girls stood dumbly and sheepishly in front of their housemother. 'This is *not* a good start to the year, girls,' went on Miss Eiseldown, crossly. 'I expect better behaviour in the evenings. A quiet game, or a book, or TV in the Junior common room.'

'Or better still, private ballet practice,' said a voice from the landing behind her. It was Amanda, looking unbearably smug.

3

Cassie Meets Miss Wrench

Cassie found it difficult to forget this embarrassing episode, especially since during the next few weeks, Amanda emerged as Miss Oakland's firm favourite in ballet class.

As the first year girls came out of class one day, and hobbled exhausted into their changing-room, Cassie reflected ruefully that not one word of praise had ever come in her own direction. Well, she'd have to do something about that, but in the meantime there were other things to worry about.

'Hey,' Cassie said to the others. 'We haven't got

those second years back for the pillow-fight yet, have we?'

Emily and some of her room-mates gathered round. 'Any suggestions?' one of them asked.

Cassie couldn't resist the idea that came into her head.

'We could put frogs or beetles or worms in their beds!'

'Yes!' enthused several of the girls.

'What if Miss Eiseldown finds out it was us?' Emily pointed out.

'She won't,' said Cassie confidently.

During their homework period later, Emily invited Cassie and Becky to her room, to discuss the plan.

'Do you think Amanda heard what we were saying in the changing-room?' asked Emily.

'I don't think so,' said Cassie. 'She was too busy grooming herself.'

'Something tells me you don't like her,' said Emily.

'Stop worrying, Em. We have to have *some* fun,' she groaned and limped around the room, holding her back in mock agony, 'after all the tortures they put us through.'

They agreed to go creepy-crawly gathering the following week, then Cassie and Becky headed back to their room.

'We'd better do some of our homework, I suppose,' said Cassie.

'Oh, it's Maths. I'd forgotten.'

'Well, don't sound so pleased,' laughed Cassie.

'I *like* Maths. It's fun.'

Cassie pulled a face at her friend. Becky paused outside their door.

'By the way,' she said 'the fruit must be nearly ripe by now. Shall I ask the cook if we can pick some for her next week?'

'That would be great! I've been dying to have a look at that ruin. Life's been just *too* hectic.' Cassie passed her hand over her brow, mock-dramatically. 'But look, Becky, let's keep it to ourselves – apart from Emily, of course.'

Half an hour later they prepared themselves for their contemporary dance class.

'It wears you out, all this changing,' complained Becky, hanging her school uniform in their shared wardrobe.

Cassie was pulling on the deep purple leggings and leotard which were the uniform for this class.

'Come on, Becky,' she said. 'It's nearly five to five and we haven't done our hair yet. We'll get done if we're late.'

They helped each other with the regulation two plaits wound round the head. Cassie always had to use gel to stop her wispy, curly bits escaping. Becky's hair was much thicker and, once secured, behaved itself. Amanda was the only one of the three who could manage the hairstyle unaided. Her shiny dark hair seemed to stay exactly where she wanted it.

33

The girls pulled on their tracksuits quickly and fastened their modern dance pumps.

'Race you!' shouted Cassie, already sprinting for the door. Becky leaped after her and they raced along the corridor and galloped down the stairs, leaving Amanda to follow rather more sedately.

Cassie turned sharp right at the foot of the stairs – and careered into Miss Wrench.

In desperate confusion, Cassie sank immediately into a curtsey, so close to the Principal that her forehead nearly touched Miss Wrench's stomach. Becky had managed to slam on the brakes behind her and was making her curtsey at a more discreet distance.

'Disgraceful,' said Miss Wrench. 'Take a black mark. You must proceed at all times in a dignified and graceful manner. You're a new girl, otherwise your punishment would certainly have been greater. Your name?'

'Cass – Cassandra Brown, Miss Wrench,' stuttered Cassie.

'Very well, Cassandra. I hope our next meeting will be less unfortunate.'

As she walked off, there was a snorting noise from behind Cassie. It was Becky, her hand to her mouth, trying to suppress her giggles. And behind her stood Amanda, looking superior.

Cassie tried to put the incident behind her in class, but she felt really upset about getting a black mark so early in her school career. Luckily, their teacher for contemporary dance was the friendly Mrs Bonsing, who could see that Cassie wasn't quite herself, but made no comment.

The majority of the class were finding a particular new movement difficult, so Mrs Bonsing asked them to imagine they were each expecting the impact of a football in their stomachs and to react accordingly. This made it much easier, especially when they were encouraged to grunt as they snapped the middle part of their bodies back. Then she taught them a sequence, built round this central movement, to the accompaniment of a jazz piece.

'I enjoyed that!' puffed Becky at the end of the class. 'But I'm absolutely starving. Half past six is just too long to wait for supper!'

'Only five minutes to go,' said Cassie. 'You'll survive.' She felt more cheerful now. 'And we're all going home this weekend. I'm so excited.'

'Me too. I'm dying to see Hammy and Button and Cotton.'

'Who are they?'

'Hammy's my hamster,' replied Becky, 'and Button and Cotton are my mice. Button's a piebald, and Cotton's white with little pink eyes and titchy pink feet.'

'Oh they sound sweet,' said Cassie. 'I've got two guinea pigs – Beethoven and Honey. They're enormous! What about you?' she asked Emily, who had just emerged from the showers. 'Have you got any pets?'

'No, none at all.'

'What are your plans this weekend?' asked Cassie.

'Oh – er – just a quiet weekend, I suppose. What's this about going fruit-picking next week?'

Cassie had noticed that Emily always clammed up whenever home was mentioned, so tactfully she didn't ask any more.

Although she hadn't felt homesick, Cassie was really looking forward to going home. When Friday came, her mum picked her up and they drove into Birmingham, stopping at a specialist dance-wear shop, where they needed to buy some extra leotards for Cassie. The girls each had to have seven ballet leotards, but the shop had only had five in Cassie's size on their last visit.

On their way back to the car from the shop, Joy Brown spotted a scrubbed-top table in the window of a small antique shop. While her mum went inside, Cassie plonked herself down in a chair outside and idly thumbed through a box of second-hand paperbacks. There was a copy of one of her favourite ballet stories. How strange to think that when she'd first read it, years before, she'd had no idea that one day she might be training to be a dancer herself. How things had changed!

Cassie suddenly felt exhausted. The first few weeks of ballet school life had been quite a challenge. Thankfully, her mum didn't stay long in the shop – the table was too expensive – and they set off again. At home, after hugging her dad and Rachel and saying hello to Adam, she went straight to her room. Everything was comfortingly familiar: a heap of cuddly toys erupted from the corner and dolls sat on every surface of the room – plastic baby dolls, china replica dolls, dolls in national costume; and books spilled on to the floor from her bookshelves.

The Browns lived in a Victorian farm cottage in a small Shropshire village. They had renovated and extended the cottage as their family had grown, so that it now had four bedrooms, a large farmhouse kitchen, a living-room and a small sitting-room. By accident, Cassie had ended up with the largest bedroom, which was a great boon to her as she could practise in it without getting in anyone else's way.

Although she had so looked forward to seeing her family again, Cassie felt far too tired to want to talk to them much that night. She went to bed very early, and woke refreshed, enjoying the feeling of being in her own comfortable bed again. She stretched luxuriously and wondered how she would spend her day. What a change from the rigorous timetable at Redwood! But as ever, once awake, she couldn't stay in bed . . .

Some time later, her brother Adam yelled up the stairs: 'Cassie, breakfast!'

Hissing with exasperation at the interruption,

she rewound her tape of Tchaikovsky's *Swan Lake* ballet music to the beginning of the particular dance she was working on. She needed to go through the sequence one more time, or else she would forget it. As she danced she felt herself *become* the swan princess, copying the fluttering arm movements she had seen ballerinas use.

In her mind's eye she was part of the woodland scene by the lake, where the swan maidens alight as dusk falls, and become human again for the duration of the night. She twizzled and leaped softly around the room, rising on demi-pointe again and again, imagining herself on full pointe. As the last cadences of the music faded away, she sank gracefully to the floor, folding her body, arms and head over her extended leg, as she had seen Anna Pavlova do, in an old film of *The Dying Swan*.

'Cassie!' yelled Adam again.

For a split second she was confused, then came out of her fantasy. 'Stop yelling, Adam!' she shouted back crossly.

She joined her family around the kitchen table.

'What have you been doing?' said Joy. 'Your porridge must be cold.'

'I called her *ages* ago,' said Adam smugly. Adam was eight and very irritating.

'*Thank you*, Adam,' said Jake, with a warning look.

After two mouthfuls of porridge, Cassie started to tell them about the dance she had been making up.

38

'It's to that bit that goes la, la-la la-la la le la la, you know, from "Swan Lake".'

'Yes, I know the tune,' said her dad, lifting his bushy eyebrows.

'Is this something you've learned at Redwood?' asked Joy.

'No,' replied Cassie with a laugh. 'It's my own idea.'

'Well, when it's ready, we'd like to see it, wouldn't we, Jake?'

'Yes indeed,' said Jake, with a little less enthusiasm, Cassie thought.

Adam pulled a face. He didn't like his sister being the centre of attention. 'Who wants to see a silly old dance?'

Rachel, the baby of the Brown household, who had been quietly getting through her breakfast, chose that moment to throw a spoonful of it at her dad, which saved Adam from a telling-off.

Rachel had just learned to walk and her confidence rather exceeded her abilities. She was very fond of climbing on the furniture and had only last week got on to the kitchen table when her mother's back was turned.

'Shall I amuse Rachel?' asked Cassie. 'I've finished eating.'

'Thanks, darling.'

'Come on little sister,' said Cassie, getting down on the floor. Rachel immediately clambered on her back and bounced up and down as if she were riding a horse. Obligingly, Cassie padded around the kitchen on all fours, with Rachel yelling, 'Ee-aw, ee-aw!' at the top of her voice.

Finally, she extricated herself from Rachel, and phoned up her old schoolfriend, Katie, to ask her round for the afternoon. Katie was in, but had already arranged to visit someone else.

Joy could tell by Cassie's face that she was disappointed.

'You must expect it, love. When you don't see people regularly, it's hard to stay in touch with them. Katie's been making new friends at the Comprehensive, just like you have at your new school. Come to think of it, you haven't told me much about Becky and . . . Emily, is it?'

So Cassie sat in the kitchen with her mother, telling her all about her first impressions of life at Redwood, and her new friends.

One thing she left out, however, was the black mark she had received from Miss Wrench. That was better forgotten.

4

Chocolate at the Ruin

'Hiya Cassie!' cried Becky, as she tumbled into their bedroom, laden with carrier bags. Her mother followed her, equally loaded.

'Hi,' answered Cassie, from the bed. 'Had a good weekend?'

'Yes, lovely thanks. The big news is that Button and Cotton *aren't* both boys after all.'

Cassie looked quizzically at Becky, who announced dramatically, 'I've got *sixteen* mice now.'

Becky's mother sighed. 'Yes, it was quite a shock. I'm glad Becky was home for the weekend. I wouldn't have known what to do with the babies.'

'Are you going to keep them all?' asked Cassie.

'That's a sore point,' said Mrs Hastings. (Becky was nodding her head vigorously behind her mother.) 'Well, there you are now, dear,' she went on, turning to kiss her daughter. 'Don't forget to work hard. This is a *wonderful* opportunity, you know.'

'Yes, Mum. I'll phone on Tuesday.'

After Mrs Hastings had left, Becky tipped the contents of one of the carrier bags on to her bed. Cassie's eyes widened – she had never *seen* so many chocolate bars and bags of sweets outside a shop.

'Don't tell me, it was your birthday,' she said.

'No, that was months ago. I just decided to blow all my pocket-money.'

'This should last you till half-term!' said Cassie.

'No, I hate saving things. Let's just get stuck in, shall we?' Becky was already unwrapping her first chocolate bar as she spoke.

'I've got a great idea!' Cassie exclaimed, jumping up. 'A midnight feast at the ruins!'

'Mmm,' agreed Becky, chomping on chocolate. 'Must ask Emily. But let's have a look at the place in daylight first – perhaps lunch-time tomorrow? What d'you think?'

Cassie nodded, a little disappointed.

'Then we could go tomorrow night, if it looked OK. We'll have to borrow a torch from someone.'

'Oh, a whole day. It's such a long time to wait,' complained Cassie.

'Well, I tell you what. There's stacks of stuff. Let's have half tonight in here, when Amanda's asleep.'

Cassie's face brightened. 'Great! I don't feel a bit tired.'

'Is Amanda back yet by the way?'

'Yes, she got back before me. She's gone off to do some private practice.' Cassie raised her eyes to the ceiling. 'That girl never stops working.'

'Well, she should sleep well then,' said Becky.

Becky's prediction was correct. After lights out at eight-thirty, it wasn't long at all until Cassie heard the note of Amanda's breathing deepen. She waited a few minutes to make sure, then crept out of her own bed to join Becky on hers. Becky had the bag hidden under the bed. She pulled it out and placed it between them.

'It's a lucky dip!' she whispered.

They had munched their way through several bars each when they both heard the ominous sound of footsteps coming towards their door. The girls froze; then Cassie came to her senses.

'Under the quilt!' she hissed.

She pushed Becky out of bed, flipped everything off the top of the quilt – chocolate, wrappers, even the half-eaten bars they had been chewing – on to Becky's sheet, and bounded back into her own bed. Becky, recovering from her surprise, quickly but gingerly lay down on top of the secret feast and pulled her quilt up to her chin.

Just in time. The door opened quietly. A head

appeared around it: Miss Eiseldown's. The light from the landing flooded in. 'Everything all right in here?' she asked. 'I thought I heard voices.'

She peered at the two innocent faces looking up at her, and then at the sleeping head of Amanda.

'Yes, we're all right, Miss Eiseldown, thank you,' breathed Cassie. Becky felt unable to speak. The sensation of sinking into sticky, melting chocolate was giving her a nearly uncontrollable urge to giggle.

'Well, be sure to settle down now. You know the rules after lights out.'

The door shut and the room was plunged into darkness once more. It was some time before the girls dared move or speak. Then, with the greatest stealth, they scooped the mess off Becky's sheet into the carrier bag.

'We'll offer this round tomorrow!' laughed Cassie. 'Genuine Becky-imprinted choccy bars!'

'Oh, *please* don't make me laugh!' warned Becky, clutching her tummy.

Poor Becky had to wait until seven the next morning to allow her pent-up laughter to explode. What eventually subdued her was having to take her chocolate-stained sheet and nightshirt to the bathroom and, with Cassie's help, scrub them clean in the bath.

Neither of them felt much like breakfast and by the time they were standing at the barre in ballet class, Cassie had developed a nagging stomach ache. She had been working hard lately in Miss Oakland's classes, but now, as the first year girls went through their pliés and tendus, ronds de jambes and grands battements, Cassie had to use every ounce of will-power to keep her mind on what she was doing.

But the greatest test came near the end of the lesson, when the jumping steps like entrechat and soubresaut were practised. Cassie's stomach just didn't want her to jump.

'Did you have some lead in your cornflakes this morning, Cassandra?' asked Miss Oakland. 'I think we'll have you doing seven entrechats and a changement on your own. AND . . .'

The music drew Cassie in relentlessly to the exercise. Although each jump was more uncomfortable than the last, she forced herself to go much higher than before. She knew that way, Miss Oakland would leave her alone. And she was right.

Unfortunately, the teacher next turned her attention to Emily.

'Why are you wearing *frayed* ballet shoes to class, Emily Pickering? I'll give you until tomorrow to get a new pair. Otherwise a black mark!'

Cassie could see that Emily was upset. After class, she made a point of being extra nice to her, but Emily had gone very quiet. Miss Eiseldown was explaining to them that the first years were expected to take up, or continue, the study of a musical instrument. Tuition was offered in piano, violin, cello, flute, clarinet and saxophone. The children were asked to choose an instrument and then Miss Eiseldown sent them along to the appropriate teacher for an aptitude test.

But Emily refused to consider learning an instrument.

'You must have a teeny interest in one of them, surely?' pressed Miss Eiseldown.

'No, I don't like music,' said Emily gruffly.

'Don't let any of your ballet teachers hear you say that!' advised her housemother.

Cassie and Becky exchanged glances. Why was Emily behaving so oddly?

The two friends both went along to meet the strings teacher, Mr Green. Becky wanted to learn cello, and Cassie violin.

The aptitude test turned out to be quite hilarious. The girls were asked to pat their heads with their left hand and rub their tummies with their right, at the same time! They both passed, despite giggling. Mr Green sorted them out an instrument each to hire and arranged their first lessons.

They proudly carried the two cases – one much larger than the other – up to their room.

'Where on earth am I going to keep this?' asked Becky, looking round the already overcrowded room.

'Under your bed?'

Luckily the bedsteads were quite high off the

floor, so that's where the new cello found a home.

'Come on, Cassie, it's lunch-time.'

'Oh, always thinking of your stomach!'

On the landing they bumped into Emily. She looked as if she had been crying.

'What's up, Em?' Cassie asked kindly.

'I'm fine,' said Emily in a stand-offish voice. Cassie looked at Becky. Becky shrugged.

'Are you coming fruit-picking with us after lunch?' she said, thinking it better to change the subject.

'Yes, do come, Emily. The cook's given us some baskets. She says she'll make some plum pies.'

Emily tried to smile. 'Yes, that sounds nice.'

Fruit-picking turned out to be just the thing to cheer her up and she soon seemed her old self again.

The plum trees were laden and the girls quickly had two full baskets picked. It was a warm September day and the picking made each of the girls feel soothed and carefree – until Cassie looked at her watch.

'It's two o'clock!' she shrieked.

'Oh no!' groaned Becky. 'It's French first. You know what Mademoiselle Beauchamp is like about being late.'

The girls each grabbed a basket and started to sprint back to school.

'We didn't even get the chance to explore the ruin,' Cassie panted as they raced to the kitchens.

'We could come back tomorrow,' said Emily.

'No, let's come back tonight. For our feast.'

'We haven't got a torch,' said Becky.

'I can borrow Jane's,' said Emily.

'Great. That's settled then!' said Cassie, as they dumped their baskets in the kitchens and set off for French.

They were forgiven for being a few minutes late for their lesson, when Becky explained to Mademoiselle what they had been doing in the grounds. Cassie felt very relieved. She hadn't wanted to get another black mark so soon after the first!

As the afternoon wore on, through French, English, double Science, homework period, and, finally, their character dance class, Cassie became more and more excited. She couldn't remember such a long afternoon. By supper-time, she felt desperate for eight-thirty to come round. By then, the house would be settled down for the night, and it would be dark enough for their adventure.

In the end, as they didn't want Amanda to suspect they were going out, they had to wait until nine o'clock for her to go to sleep. They tapped lightly on Emily's door. She came out immediately; she had been ready for over half an hour, equipped with anorak and torch. She shut her door behind her very quietly and they tiptoed along the landing. Becky carried a little bag of chocolate and sweets.

Suddenly they heard someone coming

purposefully up the stairs. They fled, as quietly as they could to the other end of the landing and hid in the recess in front of the emergency exit. Cassie peeped round the corner and saw a grey head appearing at the top of the stairs. She ducked back.

'The Wrench!' she hissed.

The girls flattened themselves against the door and held their breath. Cassie couldn't believe she was having such bad luck. First bumping into the Principal in that unbelievably clumsy manner, and now this!

She prayed that Miss Wrench wasn't going to their room for some reason, but thankfully she went past it and turned up the second flight of stairs. If she were to turn her head now, the girls would be in full view.

They kept as still as stone. Cassie's heart was banging with fear. If they were caught out of their room after lights out, they would be punished quite severely. But Miss Wrench found no reason to look behind her, and was soon safely out of sight.

'We'd better go quickly in case she comes down again,' she whispered to her friends.

'I don't feel like going down the stairs now. She might come up behind us,' said Emily.

'What about the fire-escape?' suggested Becky.

They were standing right next to it. They eased across the bolts on the door, conscious of the grating noise they were making. Luckily the door opened and closed behind them smoothly and they were out in the night air! It was quite sharp. They held their breath as they tiptoed down the metal stairs, but as careful as they were, it still made quite a ringing noise.

There was no cloud and a bright moon, so their journey across the grounds was easy. They didn't need to switch on the torch until they reached the ruin.

It was an old tower, though no longer very tall. Stones and masonry lay scattered in clumps of varying heights around it.

'I think it's a folly!' said Becky, as they walked round, studying it.

'What's a folly?' asked Cassie.

'Something foolish – you know – a building put up for no real reason – just on the whim of the owner.'

'Folly,' breathed Cassie, 'what a romantic name!'

She seized the torch from Emily and clambered inside the tower. It was open to the skies, but some of the spiral staircase still remained.

'I'm going up!' she whispered.

'Be careful!' hissed Emily. 'You don't want to twist your ankle or anything.'

'OK!' Cassie climbed as high as she could. Her head and shoulders poked out of the top of the folly and she waved cheekily to her companions over the vista from the tower.

'Hey, I can see a house in the trees, I think,' she called quietly down to Becky and Emily. She had her back to the school buildings. 'I can see a light. Do you want to come up and look?'

She lit up the steps for them with the torch and the three of them squeezed together on to the topmost unbroken stair.

'It's quite small – a cottage perhaps,' said Becky.

'And it's inside the Redwood grounds. Look, there's the boundary wall, a good way from it,' said Emily. 'Perhaps the caretaker lives there.'

'No,' said Becky. 'The caretaker's flat is at the end of the new block – you know, next to where the boys sleep.'

'Well, it's a mystery then,' announced Cassie. 'And mysteries need to be solved. Lunch-time tomorrow. What do you think?'

'Let's get back into our rooms safely first, before you start thinking up any more wild schemes,' said Emily.

'Um, haven't you both forgotten something?' asked Becky, rustling her goodies bag.

'How could we?' laughed Cassie.

They climbed down to the lower steps and Becky handed round her bag. In the evening silence, each piece of wrapping paper crackled as it was discarded, and the girls' munching sounded more like horses chomping on hay.

Becky giggled. 'If the Wrench could see us now!' she said.

'Don't say such things,' said Emily, shivering. 'I'd feel happier safely tucked up in bed.'

'You'd have missed all the excitement!' exclaimed Cassie. 'Look at the beautiful night!'

The three of them looked up. It was indeed a magnificent sight. The moon was nearly full and the whole sky was spotted with clusters of stars.

'There's the Plough!' cried Cassie, pointing. It was the only constellation she knew.

'Shh!' begged Emily. 'Don't be so noisy.'

Cassie laughed, but she was beginning to feel cold and tired. The girls picked up their litter and made their way back towards the school. They had become very quiet.

'All those sleeping people inside,' thought Cassie to herself in wonder. As they neared the girls' wing, Cassie thought she saw a dark shape move across the front wall. She blinked, but when she looked again, the shadow had gone.

'I just hope Miss Wrench is out of the way now,' whispered Emily.

'Of course she will be,' said Cassie. She sounded more confident than she felt.

However lightly they stepped, their heavy outdoor shoes clanged on the fire-escape as they went up. Cassie pushed against the door to open it.

Nothing happened.

'It's jammed!' she hissed to the others. They all put their shoulders to the door and shoved hard, but it stayed shut.

'Perhaps one of the teachers noticed the bolts

were drawn,' whispered Emily.

Becky groaned and plopped down on the top step. 'What do we do now? All the doors will be locked by this time.'

Cassie was staring at the window of the room next to the fire-escape.

'Look!' she said. 'They've left a window open. I can climb on to the window-ledge.'

'No!' cried Emily. 'You might fall!'

'It *is* a long way up,' agreed Becky.

But Cassie was already steeling herself for the climb. She found her first foothold on the bolt of a conveniently-placed drainpipe and clutched the corner of the window ledge with her left hand.

'Oh, what if the pipe comes loose!' groaned Emily.

Cassie was gulping for air. She felt very precarious, suspended mid-way between the ledge and the fire-escape. Telling herself not to panic, she waited until her heart stopped banging. Why hadn't she listened to Emily? She promised herself that she would never, *ever* do anything like this again.

Taking a huge breath, she hauled herself up on to the window-ledge – and fell in a jellyish heap on to the floor of the bedroom.

'What on earth!' exclaimed one of the occupants of the room, sitting bolt upright in bed. The other two girls were rubbing their eyes and looking about them in confusion, when the first snapped on the light.

'Shh!' pleaded Cassie. 'Don't tell Miss Eiseldown. We got locked out.'

'Oh, all right!' hissed the first girl. 'But you'd better get back to your own room, and quick!'

Her hands still shaking, Cassie quickly let herself out and unbolted the fire-door.

'All clear!' she whispered.

The others followed her on to the landing, pushing home the bolts behind them, wincing again at the creaks and squeaks. They scurried thankfully back to bed, with no one the wiser – at least as far as they knew.

5

Mrs Allingham's Cottage

The next day dawned bright and clear, but
Miss Eiseldown had to wake the three occupants
of Cassie's bedroom at seven. Cassie struggled
with herself to get out of bed. She would have
given a lot to have been allowed to sleep on
another hour or two. Becky looked even paler
than usual, and heavy-eyed. What was surprising,
though, was that Amanda looked just as tired as
they did.

'It must be all the work,' Cassie thought to herself,
rather unsympathetically.

'Sleep well?' drawled Amanda.

55

'Yes, thanks,' said Cassie. It was an odd question for Amanda to ask.

Once she had gone off to the bathroom, Cassie voiced her suspicions to Becky.

'What're you getting at, Cassie? You saw as well as I did that Amanda was fast asleep before we left the room.'

'Well, I *thought* she was asleep,' said Cassie. 'But I did think I saw a figure just ahead of us as we were coming back to school last night. Perhaps she followed us to the folly?'

'Oh I doubt it,' said Becky flatly. 'It's just your suspicious nature.'

'Oh and I suppose Mr Nobody bolted the door while we were outside!' Cassie's chin came jutting out and, for the rest of the morning, she spoke hardly a word to her friend.

But by lunch-time, Cassie had forgotten her grievance in the excitement of new plans. She was sitting with Becky and Emily in the dining hall eating macaroni cheese and salad when she broached the subject.

'Have you forgotten that we've got to catch some creepy-crawlies?' she asked.

'Of course! It's about time we got those second years back,' said Becky.

'And we could investigate that little house in the woods,' said Cassie.

'I'll come,' said Becky. 'Just wait while I have some pudding.'

As the three girls retraced their steps of the previous night, Cassie thought the folly didn't look half as mysterious in daylight. From the foot of it they could just catch a glimpse of the cottage, nearly hidden by trees.

'It's no wonder we couldn't see it from school,' said Becky.

Grubbing about at the foot of the ruins, they managed to fill an empty toffee tin with worms and a couple of slugs. Then they made their way through the trees and followed a little path which led to the cottage's garden gate.

The cottage had rambling roses and ivy spreading across its front wall and a twirling weathercock on the roof. As they got closer, they saw an elderly woman weeding the border next to a low box hedge adjoining the gate. She looked up in surprise and straightened her back, one hand pressing into the small of it.

'Hello, you must be Redwood girls. I don't often have visitors.'

She took off her gardening gloves and extended her hand to each of them in turn.

'I'm June Allingham. Pleased to meet you.'

As the three girls shyly introduced themselves, Cassie noticed her hand was wrinkled and the joints swollen with arthritis.

'Do you need any help with your garden?' Cassie asked.

'Well, how kind,' said Mrs Allingham. 'I could

use a little help. Yes. Indeed.'

Cassie looked at her friends rather sheepishly, but they smiled their agreement.

'We could come back tomorrow lunch-time?' she suggested.

'Yes, that would be very nice. If you're sure you can spare the time. I well remember how full the timetable is.' She paused, smiling dreamily. 'Now, I won't keep you today, if you're giving up your lunch break tomorrow for me. It's been very nice talking to you.'

The girls felt themselves dismissed. They said goodbye and trotted back to the lawns nearest the school where most of the Juniors congregated in their breaks.

'I wonder what connection Mrs Allingham has with Redwood?' said Cassie.

'Perhaps she's an old girl,' suggested Becky.

'I've seen her face before somewhere, but I can't think where!' said Emily.

'All will be revealed tomorrow lunch-time,' announced Cassie grandly. Her expression suddenly changed. 'Oh no. I've just thought. It's my first violin lesson!' She rushed off to her room to collect her instrument.

In fact their question was answered by breakfast-time the next day. Emily joined Becky and Cassie at their table, looking very pleased with herself.

'Guess what!' she said. 'I've found Mrs Allingham.'

'We did that yesterday,' said Becky.

'No, I mean among the photos in the hall. There's one of her. Mrs J Allingham. She was a teacher here for *years*!'

Emily's pleasure at solving the mystery was soon spoiled, however. Miss Oakland hadn't forgotten her warning of the previous day.

'Let me inspect your shoes, Emily Pickering,' she commanded, before ballet class got under way.

Emily reluctantly lifted one foot for the ballet mistress to scrutinise.

'I thought I asked you to obtain a new pair by today?'

'I've darned them, Miss Oakland, instead . . .' she trailed off weakly.

'Well, that is *not* what I asked you to do, Emily. You will have a black mark. We must keep to the highest possible standards at Redwood. It's part of the discipline of learning to be a dancer.'

Knowing that Emily had been near to tears in class, Cassie and Becky tried throughout the morning to cheer her up. But Emily stayed ominously quiet. At lunch, Becky asked her if she were still coming to Mrs Allingham's with them.

'No, you two go without me. I'm not good company.'

'Well, we only want you for your gardening skills, not to talk to,' teased Cassie but to her surprise, Emily burst into tears. 'I didn't mean it, Em. It was only a joke.'

'No, it's not you,' sniffed Emily. 'It's the ballet shoes. How can I go to class tomorrow without new ones?'

'Well, that's simple. Just march on down to the stock-room and they'll stick the new shoes on your parents' bill,' said Becky, not understanding what all the fuss was about.

But Cassie had been putting two and two together. 'Can't your mum afford them?'

'No,' said Emily, miserably. 'We had a grant at the beginning for equipment, but that's all gone now. And Mum's so hard up, I just can't ask her to buy anything else.'

Becky looked horrified. Her own parents were comfortably off and she was an only child, so there had never been any shortage of money where she was concerned.

'Come on, Em,' said Cassie, giving Emily a hug. 'We'll think of something.'

Becky's face had brightened. 'No problem!' she cried. 'Put the shoes on *my* mum's bill. I'll explain and I *know* she won't mind a bit.'

'No, don't be silly. I can't do that. Just imagine what it would do to my mum if she found out.'

'I wish I hadn't spent all my pocket-money on sweets,' moaned Becky.

'I wouldn't take it from you anyway,' Emily said quickly. 'Oh, come on!' she said. 'Let's go to Mrs Allingham's.'

A rather glum trio made its way to the cottage.

The old lady was in her garden, with the tools ready for them to do some weeding and tidying jobs for her. After they'd worked for about twenty minutes, she called them to a bench and table, where she had put a tray of home-made lemonade and soda scones.

They drank the lemonade gratefully, but Becky was the only one to take a scone.

'I'm too full of lunch still, thank you,' explained Cassie, when Mrs Allingham offered her the plate.

'Me too,' said Emily.

'You young dancers are all so skinny,' tutted Mrs Allingham. 'In my day, we had a bit of flesh on our bones.'

The girls laughed. 'Were you a dancer before you were a teacher?' asked Cassie.

The old lady nodded. 'Oh yes, indeed. I was in the corps de ballet of the Royal Ballet when Fonteyn was prima ballerina. She was lovely! And she went on dancing so long! Not like me!' She laughed.

'Did you dance at the same time as Rudolf Nureyev?' asked Cassie excitedly. He was one of her greatest heroes.

'Just the one season, before I retired from the stage. It was not long after he had defected from Russia. He was a *sensation*! We British dancers had never seen anyone jump like him in all our lives.'

She sighed and rubbed her misshapen hands together. 'I remember his Romeo to Fonteyn's Juliet. Such strength and manliness, but still managing to show the true romantic nature of the character! And Dame Margot, in her forties by then, remember, so convincing as the sweet, innocent fifteen-year-old Juliet. Together, they were just . . . remarkable. Quite remarkable.'

As she broke off and sighed again, Becky took a peek at her watch. It was time to go. Mrs Allingham thanked them and invited them to visit her any time they wanted to. Then she shakily took out three pound coins from an old black purse on the table.

'Now, here's a little pocket-money for you.'

Cassie hadn't expected any payment, but was just about to thank her for it, when Emily intervened.

'Oh no, Mrs Allingham. We really couldn't. We've enjoyed helping you and listening to your wonderful tales.'

Cassie swallowed her words and they said their goodbyes and returned to school.

'You needed that money,' Cassie said to Emily on their way back.

'It wouldn't have been right to take it!' insisted Emily. 'She might be really poor.'

'Well, you're just going to have to get some new shoes somehow!'

As they joined the orderly lines of boys and girls streaming into classrooms, Amanda came up to them.

'Where've you been sneaking off to?' she asked.

Cassie gave warning looks to the others. She wanted to keep Mrs Allingham their secret.

'Just a stroll to the orchard,' she answered.

Amanda shrugged her shoulders rather huffily and said no more. During the next lesson, Emily leaned across to Cassie and whispered in her ear.

'I've decided what to do. I'll get a pair from the stock-room. Mum won't get the bill till the end of term. By then, I'll have saved up all my school pocket-money, and I'll earn some more in the half-term holiday, doing a paper round or something.'

Cassie felt pleased that Emily was finding a way round her problem. But at the rate at which students wore through their ballet shoes, she very much doubted that Emily's savings would keep pace with her bill.

Cassie had something else on her mind as well: a tin full of creepy-crawlies. She hadn't had a chance yet to get to the second years' beds when no one was around.

Just then the English teacher asked the class to get out their copies of *A Christmas Carol* and Cassie discovered she hadn't brought hers in her bag.

Here's my chance! she thought, thrusting her hand into the air.

'What is it, Cassandra?' asked Miss Pointer.

'May I be excused to go and fetch my copy from my room, please?' she asked politely.

Permission granted, she rushed upstairs. The landing was silent and empty. She took out from her desk first the book and secondly the tin of worms . . .

6

An Ill-timed Injury

Waiting for lights out that night seemed endless.
When at last the time came, everything happened
very quickly. Within sixty seconds of Cassie's
climbing into bed, the landing resounded with
shrieks and yells. Cassie and Becky burst into
laughter. Their plan had worked.

They couldn't help noticing, however, that the
shrieks were getting louder. And *nearer*.

Suddenly all eight occupants of the second-year
dormitory burst in and flung handfuls of worms
into the room. Unfortunately, most of them landed
on Amanda's bed. Amanda's yells were the loudest

Cassie had ever heard from anyone.

It was no surprise when Miss Eiseldown appeared in her dressing-gown, looking even crosser than when she had stopped the pillow-fight.

'Girls, *girls*, what *is* going on?'

Amanda, who had quickly regained her composure, accused the second years of bursting in and showering her with worms. Eventually though, the whole story came out and Miss Eiseldown wasn't too pleased with any of them, excepting (of course) Amanda.

'Cassandra and Rebecca, if I hear another *peep* out of you this term, you'll be for the high jump. However, I view the behaviour of you second years in a much more serious light. As you very well know, you are placed on the first-year landing to befriend and guide the new girls. You will all be placed in detention. Come and see me first thing tomorrow morning.'

When all was calm again, Cassie lay back in bed, feeling very lucky indeed to have been let off so lightly. She remembered with some relief that she was going home for the half-term holiday the following evening – relief, tinged with a little sadness at saying goodbye to her friends. She had spent so much time in their company recently that she knew she would miss them.

On Friday evening, Emily was first to be collected

and Cassie privately wished her luck in finding a holiday job.

On the journey back to Shropshire, Cassie remembered how tired she'd felt on her first weekend home. She must be building up stamina, she thought. At home, she spent a good hour chatting to her mum about school, and was allowed to stay up to watch a film on TV. This was a real treat, after all those early bedtimes. Her brother Adam wasn't too impressed, however, as he had to go to bed before the film finished.

'We'll video the end for you,' Joy Brown promised.

'It's not *fair*,' moaned Adam, 'soon as *she* gets home she gets a stay-up night!'

Joy ignored this comment and escorted her protesting son upstairs. The next morning, Adam seemed to have 'got out of bed on the wrong side', as his dad put it. Whether he was resentful about his earlier bedtime, or just finding it difficult to adjust to Cassie's being home again, his behaviour to Cassie was pretty dreadful. She didn't help matters by trying to boss him about at every opportunity and making it quite clear that *she* was grown up, now she lived away from home, while *he* was still a silly little boy.

Adam got worse and worse all week. Cassie was growing increasingly bored – she just wasn't used to having nothing to do. Their parents' patience was stretched to the limit. Only Rachel went on in her usual sweet, but noisy, way, unaffected by the other two squabbling children.

Jake took Adam off fishing for a couple of afternoons, while Joy and Cassie went shopping and took Rachel to the park, which eased the tension, but on the Friday, when Cassie had invited her old school-friend, Katie, round for the day, Adam had nothing to do. All his friends were busy and his dad had to go into school to prepare work for the following week.

'My brother's such a pain,' Cassie complained to Katie, while they were playing records in her bedroom.

'He can't be as bad as mine!' said Katie. 'Yesterday, he ate the middle bit of a jumbo felt-tip pen, and his poo turned green!'

'Oh no!' yelled Cassie laughing uncontrollably. 'But he *is* only two,' she said, when she could get her breath.

'What's so funny?' asked Adam bursting into the room.

'You should knock first and wait to be invited in,' Cassie said, in a lofty tone.

'Come on, what's the joke?'

'None of your business,' said Cassie. 'Now, scat!'

Adam went out, muttering under his breath, only to reappear ten minutes later, holding a plate of biscuits.

'This must be a peace-offering!' said Cassie.

'And he knocked,' said Katie.

'Mum told me to bring you these,' said Adam innocently.

'Ooh, fancy ones. We only usually have digestive,' said Cassie.

She let Katie make her choice first. Her friend bit into the Jammy Dodger she'd chosen – only to find the biscuit was rubber.

Adam tried to make a quick exit, but not quick enough. Cassie tackled him, and he, the plate and the fake biscuits all went flying. Then the two girls sat on him till he apologised.

After that, Adam left them in peace.

'We seem to have got rid of your brother,' said Katie later in the afternoon.

'I wouldn't be too sure of that.'

Cassie heard her mother calling them to wash their hands ready for tea. There was a new block of white soap in the bathroom wash-basin. Cassie thought it smelt a bit strange when she picked it up, but as she started to lather her hands with it, she dropped it in horror.

'Look, Katie! My hands are filthy!' They stared at her hands in disbelief.

'It's trick soap!' concluded Katie.

'Adam again! Oh well, let's use some shampoo to get it off with. I'm not going to give him the satisfaction of knowing I fell for his stupid trick. *And* I'll pinch his soap and hide it!'

Cassie spent her meal-time hatching plans to get Adam back. Katie had to go home just after tea, so

Cassie was left alone to play a trick on her brother. She decided to go and hide in his wardrobe until he came up to his room. She waited for a few minutes, squashed in the muffled darkness of hanging clothes, and then heard him come in. She counted silently to ten. She could hear Adam sorting through some magazines on his desk.

Now! she thought, launching herself out of the wardrobe and shrieking at the top of her voice. She had the pleasure of seeing Adam's face whip round, a deathly white colour, before landing agonisingly on the floor. She crumpled over her ankle, her shrieks authentic now, and her parents came running upstairs to see what was the matter.

'I've broken my ankle!' she sobbed, in her father's arms. Jake's strong hands probed the joint.

'No, I don't think so,' he said. 'It's probably a sprain.'

This verdict was confirmed later by the family doctor, who said she must rest her leg as much as possible. There would certainly be no dancing for several weeks.

This was nothing short of catastrophic. Cassie sobbed and sobbed on the car-journey home, despite her mum's assurances that the time would pass quickly and she would soon be as strong as ever.

She went back to Redwood on the following Sunday evening, with a heavy heart and a doctor's note, explaining her injury. The next morning, after lots of sympathy and kind words from her friends – even from Amanda – she showed the note to Miss Oakland at the start of the class.

'This is most unfortunate timing, Cassandra. From tomorrow, Madame Larette will be taking your ballet class, leading up to an inspection class by Miss Wrench. I can only suggest you get changed as normal and attend all your classes. Listening and watching, you will still learn something.'

Not a flicker of a smile, a hint of sympathy. Cassie wondered how she could be so hard-hearted. But at the end of the class, when the others had been dismissed, Miss Oakland asked Cassie to stay behind. It was as though she suddenly let a mask drop away from her face. Cassie could now see her genuine concern, as she questioned her about the sprain. Perhaps she was human after all.

Cassie felt very disappointed that she would not be joining in Madame Larette's classes. Everyone loved the warm French woman who was the school's principal ballet mistress. She had been forewarned of Cassie's condition, and had a surprise for her, and the rest of the class, when they arrived in the studio next morning. There were gym-mats all over the floor.

'We shall start, *mes chéries,* with a few exercises I learned at the Kirov.'

Cassie beamed when she was invited to join in the floor-work, which was quite similar, she thought, to some of her mum's yoga postures.

Madame Larette positioned herself next to Cassie's mat and fussed over her throughout the exercises. It was such a change from Miss Oakland, whose little crumbs of praise always fell in Amanda's lap. Cassie wondered if it was this change which brought about what happened next.

Amanda suddenly cried out, during a back-bending exercise, and complained to Madame that she had pulled a muscle.

'Oh, *ma pauvre!*' said Madame, rushing to her side. 'You must leave *maintenant,* and rest.'

When Amanda had left the room, she addressed the class.

'Please don't strain or jerk in the exercises. We don't want any more injuries, *merci beaucoup.*'

After class, in the changing rooms, Becky said more or less what Cassie was thinking.

'A bit of copy-cat-itis there, I think!'

When Cassie agreed, Emily chided them both for being so uncharitable.

'Oh, come on, Emily,' Cassie insisted, 'Amanda's always so loose, especially in her back.'

'Yes,' said Becky, 'she just didn't like Cassie having all the attention.'

They were proved right when, in the evening, Cassie caught sight of Amanda practising on her own in one of the practice rooms. She rushed upstairs to tell Emily what she had seen. Emily was in her dormitory, darning a hole in her tights.

'I still think you're a bit hard on Amanda. I know she's stuck up and everything, but you could be friendlier.'

Cassie blushed and Emily quickly changed the subject.

'Is this darn neat enough do you think?'

'Yes, much better than I could do. Not even Miss Oakland's eagle eyes will spot that!'

Cassie suddenly remembered she hadn't asked Emily about her holiday.

'Did you manage to get a paper round?'

'No, it was far too short a time. But I *did* get a job, helping next door with Mrs Edward's children. They're only little and she's always busy, so she paid me to amuse them for an hour a day.'

'Oh great, Emily. I am pleased.'

Emily frowned. 'It's not just *one* pair of shoes, though, is it?'

'Don't worry. It'll all work out.'

'I hope so. It's not working out too well at home though. My mum's *so* tired, doing an evening job and looking after my little brothers and sisters.'

'How many have you got?'

'Four. The youngest – Sam – is only five months.'

'Quite a handful!' Cassie had never plucked up courage before to ask Emily so much about her home-life. She knew Emily didn't like talking about it.

'I help Mum as much as I can when I'm there – but, well, I'm just not there very much now, am I?'

'Doesn't your Dad take the kids out now and then?' Cassie knew several children whose parents were separated and whose dads gave them a wonderful time every other weekend.

'No,' said Emily. Cassie could tell by her tone, that she had asked one question too many. And she saw that her friend's eyes were full of tears.

Cassie felt glum about missing out on so much dancing, although one consolation was that she was getting more violin practice done for Mr Green. Madame Larette had continued to begin each class with Kirov type exercises, for which Cassie felt very grateful. At least she wouldn't stiffen up completely.

'Madame's a real sweetie,' she commented after ballet class one morning. 'I'm sure she only included those floor exercises for my benefit.'

'I wouldn't be a bit surprised,' said Emily. 'How's your ankle feeling now?'

'It doesn't hurt so much when I put a bit of weight on it.'

'We'll have you galloping around again before you know it!' laughed Becky. 'Are you up to a visit to you-know-who at lunch-time?' She was careful what she said, as Amanda was within earshot.

'Great idea,' said Cassie. 'But I've got to go to the laundry room first.'

In the end she decided to call in for her laundry, before going to the dining hall, to save time. She picked up the neat pile of washed and pressed garments with her name on and hurriedly took them back to her room. She flung them on the bed, intending to put them away later, and noticed immediately that there were only four pink leotards there, instead of five.

Cassie thought no more about it until she was halfway through her steamed pudding at lunch. A group of first year boys at the other side of the hall had begun waving something pink on the end of a long stick.

'What on earth are they waving a flag for?' asked Becky.

'It's not a flag. It's a leotard!' said Emily.

With a shock, Cassie realised whose leotard it must be. The 'flag' was lowered before any teachers spotted it. Cassie charged over to the boys' table, flanked by Emily and Becky.

'Where did you get that leotard?' Cassie demanded. She knew the boys – their names were Matthew, Tom, Gregory and Ernst – but had never really spoken to them before. This didn't stop her from talking to them now as she did to her younger brother, Adam, when he had played some trick on her.

'Come on, I'm waiting,' she said, hands on hips. The boys were giggling their heads off.

'Matthew,' she said, turning on the tallest boy, who, she suspected, was the ringleader. 'I asked you *where* you got that leotard?'

Cassie was by now bright red and at the point of exploding.

'Let's have a look at it,' said Becky, snatching the leotard off the stick. She read the name label. 'Cassandra Brown!'

'Come on, Cassie, let's go. They're not worth it!' said Emily, pulling her friend away.

'Yes,' agreed Becky. 'Here's your leotard, all in one piece. Let's go.'

Despite feeling very angry, Cassie let her friends lead her away. It was difficult to make a dignified exit, however, hobbling on a sprained ankle.

Even though they took the walk across the grounds very slowly, by the time they reached Mrs Allingham's cottage, Cassie's ankle was throbbing painfully. The old lady was full of sympathy and insisted that Cassie came inside to rest while the other two dug up some gladioli bulbs for her. It was the first time Cassie had been inside the cottage and she was surprised at its loveliness. Mrs Allingham always dressed so simply, but her house was adorned with frilly curtains, embroidered cushions and richly patterned rugs. It was an Aladdin's cave, with nearly every wall festooned with paintings and hangings, and every surface bursting with ornaments.

'Now, let me get you something to help that ankle,' said Mrs Allingham, rummaging through one of her dresser drawers. 'Ah, here it is – arnica – wonderful for injuries.'

Cassie looked rather doubtfully at the white tablet which Mrs Allingham was offering her.

'There's nothing to worry about. It can't hurt you at all. You could give it to a baby. Homeopathic, you know.'

As the tablet dissolved in Cassie's mouth, Mrs Allingham regaled her with more stories about her dancing days.

'And then there was the time I got the chance to dance Giselle. I was the understudy really, but the principal dancer – her name was Alicia Smerkova – was ill that night.'

'Was it very exciting?' Cassie asked, wide-eyed.

'It was disastrous. Quite disastrous. The tombstone I was hiding behind at the beginning of Act Two fell over! There I was, crouching down, looking far from wraith-like. The audience laughed, I'm afraid.'

'Oh no, that would have put me off completely!'

'I felt terrible, inside, but I tried very hard not to let it show in my dancing. That's what being professional is all about, dear.'

'So did the performance go well, after that?'

'Yes and no. Most of it went very well, but nearly at the end of Act Two, which is the final act of the ballet, my partner landed badly after a grand jeté en tournant, and – you'll like this bit – sprained his ankle.'

Cassie laughed. It was good to know that others had shared her misfortune.

'So there you are,' said Mrs Allingham. 'We all have our little problems.'

'Yes, you're right,' said Cassie. 'But at the moment, it's really getting me down.'

'Oh, in a couple more weeks, you'll forget you've ever had a sprain.'

Mrs Allingham made the girls a mug of hot chocolate each and after she had taken Becky's and Emily's outside to them, she sat down again with a cup of tea for herself.

'Emily looks to me as if she has a few problems too,' she said, her voice full of concern.

Cassie nodded. She felt she could confide in the kind old lady. 'She's worrying about her mum a lot, I do know that. There are four other children and no dad around. But I don't know the details.'

'Well, the best thing she can do is work hard here and stop worrying about her mother. Her mother's old enough to look after herself.'

'It's not just that though,' Cassie went on. 'They're *very* hard up and Emily has no money to buy extra equipment, ballet shoes and things.'

'Ah, now that *is* more worrying. Yes indeed.'

Mrs Allingham had just sat back in her chair to ponder this latest information when there was a knock on the door.

'That'll be my visitor,' she said, rising to answer it. She showed a tall, silvery-haired man into the sitting-room and introduced him to Cassie.

'Mr Flint and I share an interest in antiques. We

met a few weeks ago at a saleroom. Here we are, look.' She moved across the room and lifted up a pretty jug from the dresser. 'We were both bidding for this lovely little piece of lustreware.'

'And Mrs Allingham won!' exclaimed Mr Flint. His blue eyes twinkled as he laughed. Cassie tried to take a good look at him, without appearing rude. She had the uncomfortable feeling that she had seen him before, but she couldn't remember where.

'Do you like my other bits and pieces, Cassandra?' Mrs Allingham asked, indicating the dresser. It was crowded with china ornaments, jugs, vases and a pewter tea service.

'Yes, they're lovely.'

'Each one tells a story. I don't know much about antiques really, but I know what I like. And when I used to travel a bit more than I do now, I would always bring some pretty little thing home with me.'

Cassie limped over to the dresser for a closer look. 'Where did you buy this?' she asked, pointing to a china egg with a figure nestling in it. 'It's beautiful.'

'Pick it up. Don't be afraid. It came from a little shop attached to a doll museum, down in South Wales.'

Mr Flint had also come over to the dresser. 'Quite lovely,' he said, turning it upside down. 'And exquisitely painted.' As he handled the ornament, Cassie saw his pale blue eyes light up with interest.

The conversation was interrupted when Becky

and Emily knocked on the door. Mrs Allingham asked them into the sitting-room and they looked around, as Cassie had done previously, in surprise and wonder.

'We'd better get back, Cassie,' said Emily at last. 'To allow you enough time.'

'Yes, I'm a real slowcoach at the moment,' said Cassie, laughing. Her ankle was feeling much better; was it the sit-down, or the arnica tablet, she wondered? 'Goodbye, Mrs Allingham. And thanks for everything.'

Mrs Allingham smiled at her and Cassie knew she was thinking again about Emily's plight.

'I was glad of your company,' she said.

As they made their way slowly back to school, Cassie pondered again about where she had seen Mr Flint before. The memory was as elusive as an escaped pet rabbit. But somehow she knew it mattered – there was something not quite right about Mr Flint . . .

'Hey, that's Amanda, isn't it?' cried Becky. 'She just went behind that tree.'

But by the time the girls reached the tree in question, there was nobody there, and no way of knowing if Amanda had been snooping on them or not.

7

Hallowe'en

Hallowe'en was approaching and Cassie had taken the precaution of bringing to school in her suitcase an old white sheet, a wire coat-hanger and the dirty soap which she had 'borrowed' from her brother. She was looking forward to putting these items to good use.

Her ankle felt fine. She had had a visit from the school's visiting orthopaedic consultant. He was pleased with the way it was healing but forbade her to dance on it just yet.

'Oh, it's *so* annoying!' she complained to Becky as they made their way in their red tracksuits to ballet class one morning. 'I'm just going to be completely out of practice!'

'I don't know what you're moaning about,' countered Becky. 'I wouldn't mind having a rest from ballet class for a few weeks!'

After floor exercises, Cassie sat on a chair by the piano and watched Madame's class. Her eyes were constantly drawn towards Amanda. She could see why Miss Oakland had always showered her with praise. Amanda really was in a class of her own. Cassie wondered if she had 'star quality' – something ballet teachers were supposed to be able to spot. Her gaze wandered around the rest of the class; Becky was quite competent in her technique, but always looked bored. Emily was probably the best dancer after Amanda. She had a good classical line, but lacked Amanda's confidence and attack. And, thought Cassie rather sadly, her ballet uniform did always look rather worn and tatty.

Before the girls were asked to make their curtseys, Madame Larette announced that Miss Wrench would be coming to take her inspection class next week, to judge their progress.

' 'Er bark is worse than 'er bite, *mes chéries*,' she exclaimed, when she noticed the looks of horror on most faces. 'Just remember, *dance* your best and *look* your best. No untidiness please.'

Madame took Emily on one side as the others left the studio. Cassie overheard her ask her friend to wear her best practice clothes for the inspection class, and to get some new tights and shoes from the stock-room.

'Yes, Madame,' said Emily, but Cassie noticed how pale she had become.

The next day was October 31st. Cassie had a violin lesson that lunch-time, so Becky and Emily promised not to make any Hallowe'en preparations without her.

Mr Green was very pleased with her progress. She had learned two new pieces in a week and could play them with hardly any mistakes.

'You are very musical, Cassandra,' he told her. 'Keep up the practice, and we'll soon have you joining the school orchestra.'

Cassie privately wondered how she'd find the time to take part in the school orchestra, but was flattered by his praise.

The afternoon's lessons seemed particularly boring and Cassie was glad when the time for character class came round, even though she wasn't able to join in. By the end of the class, however, she was itching to get on to her feet and dance the tarantella, which Mrs Bonsing had been teaching the other girls and boys.

Cassie had been watching Matthew in the group – the tall boy who had taken her leotard from the laundry-room. Emily had discovered something very interesting about him: apparently he had never been to a ballet lesson in his whole life, before auditioning for Redwood. He had been told he had the perfect physique for a dancer. The information hadn't made Cassie like him any better – in fact, at that very moment, she felt very cross with him indeed.

A rather black mood seemed to have descended on her. At supper, Becky was the only cheerful one of the threesome.

'What's up with you two?' she asked.

'I'm just fed up with sitting out in every class,' moaned Cassie. 'I won't be at all ready for the Wrench.'

'Oh, you're a brilliant dancer, Cassie,' said Becky. 'You'll be fine.'

'No I won't,' said Cassie.

'At least you've got something decent to wear,' Emily broke in.

'I thought you'd found a way round that problem?' asked Becky.

'I've already booked three pairs of shoes. I just *can't* put anything else on the bill. I'll never be able to pay for it.'

'Oh, look, have my pocket-money,' said Becky. 'Mum gave me quite a lot over half-term, and I've only spent a bit.'

'You know I can't,' said Emily.

'Or *won't!*' scoffed Cassie.

'What do you mean?'

'If you weren't so proud, you'd let other people help you,' Cassie said impatiently.

'I don't *want* other people to help me!' cried Emily.

'You're just daft, Emily. If you'd told Miss Eiseldown, I'm sure she'd have sorted some money out for you.'

'I tell you, I don't want other people's charity!'

'Don't be stupid. Go and share your problem with one of the teachers.'

'Oh, I'm amazed you even know I've *got* a problem,' Emily snapped. 'All you ever think about is your stupid ankle!'

Cassie's cheeks flamed as though she'd been stung. She banged her knife and fork down on the table.

'And all *you* do is whinge and snivel all the time, like a spoiled brat! I really *hate* you, Emily!'

Emily pushed her plate away from her and stormed out of the dining hall. Heads had been turning towards the raised voices. Cassie suddenly felt very self-conscious.

'You've really upset her now,' said Becky, helplessly.

'She's upset *me*!' said Cassie.

'I know, but Emily's got a lot to worry about.'

Cassie's chin jutted forward and Becky knew it was useless to say any more. Back in their bedroom, Cassie felt all the fun of Hallowe'en had been spoilt; she felt like crying. But Becky was very nice to her and tempted her with crazier and crazier ideas, so that by the time Amanda came into the room, she

85

felt more like her old cheerful self.

Amanda was carrying a large turnip, which she proceeded to hollow out with a knife and spoon. She had also brought in a candle, matches and string.

'What are you making?' asked Becky.

'A turnip lantern. What does it look like?' said Amanda.

'Sorry I asked,' said Becky. 'Come on, Cassie, let's take our "equipment" down the landing.'

Becky had already draped Cassie's old white sheet over the wire coat-hanger. The girls strung up the sheet on the landing and Becky remained standing on a chair, holding their 'ghost' at the highest point of the string, while Cassie knocked on the second years' door.

As soon as the door opened, Becky let the 'ghost' go. It slid down the string past the second years' room, producing shrieks of fright and laughter.

'Who are we going to play the dirty soap trick on?' asked Cassie.

'How about Amanda?' suggested Becky. 'It would be easiest to sneak the soap on to our washbasin.'

The girls went back into their room with this plan in mind. Becky was to engage Amanda in conversation, while Cassie switched the soaps.

'Your lantern's looking great, Amanda,' said Becky.

'Oh thanks. I'll light the candle and switch the light off. It should be quite effective, I think.'

Cassie gave a grin at the mention of turning the light off. That was just the opportunity she needed. As the eerie face of the turnip lantern glowed in the dark room, Amanda picked it up by the string handle she'd made and moved towards the door.

'Going to show Emily and Miranda and that lot, are you?' asked Becky, disappointed that she was leaving without washing her hands.

'No,' said Amanda curtly.

'Where *are* you going then?' asked Cassie.

'Trick-or-treating, of course. It's Hallowe'en, remember?'

'But *where* are you going trick-or-treating?'

'That's *my* business.'

She closed the door behind her smartly and Becky and Cassie heard her going downstairs.

'I don't like it,' said Cassie.

'Neither do I,' said Becky.

'You don't think . . .' But Cassie didn't have to finish her sentence. It was obvious Becky had had the same thought. They left the room hurriedly, hoping to catch up with Amanda.

They caught sight of her next in the grounds and stayed a discreet distance behind her. The turnip lantern marked her out quite clearly.

'She's taking quite a risk,' whispered Cassie. 'You could easily spot that lantern from school.'

'She certainly seems to be heading for Mrs Allingham's.'

'She *must* have followed us there at least once.'

'Probably more than once,' Becky replied. 'D'you think we'd better stop her?'

'Yes, I do!' said Cassie. 'It could frighten poor old Mrs Allingham out of her wits.'

Having made up their minds to stop Amanda, they tracked her until she was well into the orchard. They thought they would be better screened there from school. Amanda had not looked behind her once. Becky and Cassie had gained ground and hid themselves behind a tree. Cassie squeezed her friend's hand as a signal. They sprinted forwards and, before Amanda had time to realise what was happening, had seized her arms.

'Not a step further, Miss Renwick,' cried Cassie theatrically.

'What's going on?' shouted Amanda, struggling to get free.

'It's all right,' said Becky. 'We don't want to hurt you. We just don't want you to go and frighten Mrs Allingham, that's all.'

'Oh, is that what her name is?' said Amanda. 'You've kept it all very quiet, haven't you?'

'We didn't mean any harm,' said Cassie. 'It was just our little secret – visiting her.'

'Well, I don't see why you should be trying to stop *me* visiting her,' said Amanda.

'We've told you, Amanda. You might frighten her. She hasn't any neighbours around. It could be quite scary, hearing a knock on the door at this time of night.'

'All right then, have it your own way. But not everyone's as wimpish as you!' Amanda pulled her arms free, blew out the lantern, and stalked off back towards the school.

'Shall we just go a bit further into the woods?' asked Cassie, on impulse. It was a fine, starry night, and she felt somehow reluctant to go back into the confines of the ballet school.

'I don't know,' said Becky, warily. 'It'll be much darker under the trees.'

'Just a *little* way,' pleaded Cassie.

'OK then.'

They fumbled onwards and reached a point on the path, where normally Mrs Allingham's cottage became visible in the daytime. The darkness had deepened considerably, and it was pleasant to see a light ahead, shining from one of the windows.

'We'd better go back now,' said Becky. 'It must be well after lights out.'

As they turned away from the light, they heard the cottage door opening and the sound of voices. They stood quite still, listening. Had Amanda somehow got past them? They identified Mrs Allingham's voice. The other voice was a man's.

'Mr Flint again,' whispered Cassie. 'Will he come this way?'

'No, he'll go the other way, out of the gate in the wall at the back of the wood.'

Cassie breathed a sigh of relief. She felt glad when they re-emerged on to the open lawns. The woods had been a little *too* dark, although she wouldn't have admitted it to Becky. The night sky above them let her mind and spirit open upwards.

She burst into a little dance that sent her running and leaping in the starlight. At last Becky grew impatient and they hurried back to school. The side door from which they'd left their wing was still open. It wasn't normally locked until about half past nine. Once they were in the building, they had to be extremely careful not to be seen. There were still a few members of staff around at that time of night, but luckily, they didn't meet any of them.

'I remember reading about something you can do on Hallowe'en to find out who you're going to marry,' whispered Cassie, as they slipped along their landing. They let themselves into their bedroom quietly and found that Amanda was already fast asleep.

'What do you have to do?' asked Becky.

'You sit in front of a mirror at midnight, by candle-light, and the face of your future husband should appear, by magic.'

'Well, it's past nine already,' said Becky. 'Do you think we could stay awake that long?'

Somehow, the girls managed it, though not without difficulty. They borrowed Amanda's turnip-lantern, for the candle-light, and positioned themselves in front of the mirror, ready for midnight.

'I feel a bit scared,' admitted Cassie, with a giggle.

'If a face that wasn't mine *really* appeared, I'd die of fright.'

'Me too,' said Becky, with feeling. She checked her watch. Twelve o'clock was just approaching. The girls stared intently into the glass at their reflections, which flickered strangely in the lantern-light.

Suddenly, a third face appeared in the centre of the mirror. A face with wide eyes and open mouth.

There was an unearthly scream. Cassie and Becky both shot off the chair, shrieking, before they realised it was just Amanda, sitting up in bed behind them.

'You idiots!' she cried. 'You terrified me!'

'And you frightened us, too!' laughed Cassie. They all dissolved into helpless giggles, which they quickly suppressed when they heard Miss Eiseldown's footsteps outside.

'Oh no!' groaned Becky.

But Cassie had already thought of a plan. She blew out the candle and sat herself on the bed, with her arm around Amanda. Becky frowned. What was going on?

As Miss Eiseldown entered, Cassie could be heard saying, 'It's all right, Amanda, it's all right . . .'

'What on earth was that awful scream?' asked their housemother. 'I thought someone was getting murdered, at least.'

'Amanda just had a nightmare,' said Cassie. 'It woke us both up.'

'Oh I see,' said Miss Eiseldown, sitting herself

down on the other side of Amanda. 'Are you all right now, dear?'

Cassie crossed her fingers behind her back. She hoped Amanda wouldn't give the game away.

'Yes, I'm fine now, Miss Eiseldown. Thank you,' replied Amanda meekly. 'Sorry for waking everybody up.'

'Well, goodnight, girls. Let's hope we get through to morning without any more disturbances.'

After she'd left, Amanda got out of bed and hid the turnip-lantern and box of matches.

'Thanks for not telling on us,' said Becky.

Amanda gave them a rare smile, before turning out the light.

8

The Inspection Class

When Cassie woke next morning, before the call from Miss Eiseldown, the first thing she thought of was the row with Emily. She wondered if they would ever be friends again and if Emily could forgive her for the horrible things she had said. The excitement of Hallowe'en had pushed it to the back of her mind for a while, but now she felt thoroughly gloomy at the prospect of Emily not speaking to her.

She sat up and saw that Becky was still asleep. Amanda was already moving about the room. Thank goodness Amanda had decided to go along with her story about the nightmare. Although, if she hadn't, Cassie would have been able to tell a few tales about *her*. As it was, Cassie felt more friendly towards Amanda than she had done since the beginning of term. She was about to speak to her, when she saw her go across to the wash-basin and turn on the tap for a wash.

The wash-basin! Cassie felt hot and cold at the same time. It was too late to warn her. She had already lathered the trick soap on to her face and hands. Cassie winced and put her head under the quilt as Amanda turned on her furiously.

'My face is all dirty!' she yelled.

'Sorry, Amanda,' said Cassie meekly, peeping over her quilt. 'I forgot I'd put the trick soap there.'

'A likely story!' snorted Amanda. 'I'll get you back for this. Just you wait!'

Becky was by now wide awake and took in the situation immediately.

'It was only meant to be a Hallowe'en joke, Amanda. We just forgot it was still there, that's all.'

Amanda snorted again. 'I suppose this is your idea of *fun*,' she said. 'It's just like being with a pair of infants, sneaking off all the time, playing silly tricks.'

'Well, you were up to a pretty silly trick yourself last night,' Cassie reminded her.

Amanda turned on her heel and left the room with an expression of complete disdain on her face.

Becky sighed. 'Oops,' she said. 'Well, it can't be

94

helped. We'd better get up.'

'Oh, I've just remembered,' said Cassie. 'I've another appointment with the doctor this morning. I'd better get down to breakfast early, because it's first thing.'

The flurry of activity made her feel more cheerful. And Mr Perkins' verdict made her more cheerful still. She was to be allowed to join in class from that very day!

It was wonderful to be dancing again. She enjoyed every minute of Madame Larette's ballet class that morning, even though she knew how out of practice she had become. But then, at the end of the lesson, Madame informed them that Miss Wrench's inspection class had been brought forward to that afternoon, as she was going to be too busy the following week.

This news threw Cassie into a panic. She was terribly under-prepared. To make matters worse, Emily avoided her at break and at lunch-time, and Amanda kept throwing her dirty looks. Dirty looks to match her dirty face, thought Cassie to herself with an inward, guilty giggle. Although Amanda had scrubbed and scrubbed, grubby patches still remained on her skin.

Miss Wrench was waiting beside the piano as the girls filed into Studio One. She looked austere as always, dressed in a white blouse and grey, finely-pleated skirt. Her usual black lace-ups had been replaced by a pair of white teaching shoes. She was holding a short stick, which Cassie had never noticed her carrying before. Once the first years were all in the room, she tapped her stick on the floor, as if calling for attention. This was hardly necessary, thought Cassie, as the girls were standing in complete silence.

They warmed up with a polka step around the room and then went to the barre. Cassie felt nervous and tired. Her late night was catching up with her. Quite quickly, errors crept into her exercises. Miss Wrench didn't say anything, but Cassie knew she had noticed, nevertheless.

The Principal saved up her criticisms until they were working in the centre. She didn't like their développés; their pas de chats weren't crisp enough. She had everyone doing four pas de chats and changement, individually. One by one, the girls felt the lash of her tongue. No one could please her. When Cassie's turn came, she had her heart in her mouth.

As Miss Wrench studied her, Cassie remembered, with some discomfort, the time she had bumped into her in the corridor.

'No, no, young lady,' cried Miss Wrench. 'One of your feet is lazy. You're just not stretching it.'

The foot in question was, of course, the weak ankle. Cassie started to explain. 'Miss Wrench, I spr—'

But she was interrupted. 'Do not speak in class,' thundered Miss Wrench, 'unless you are asked a question. That is one rule I will *not* have broken.'

She peered more closely at Cassie through her large spectacles. 'Cassandra Brown, isn't it? Yes, I remember you.'

Amanda was next. Her pas de chats were faultless. Cassie felt sick with envy and resentment.

'*Thank* you, Amanda,' said Miss Wrench, in a much warmer tone than Cassie had ever heard her use before. 'That was very good.'

Emily was the last of the girls to perform the exercise. Cassie thought she looked nervous and unhappy. She wished she could have put the clock back to the morning of the previous day, before their silly argument. Becky had been right, she saw that now. She just hadn't made enough allowances for Emily's worries.

Considering the strain she was under, which showed in her face, Emily's work, as always, was exact and beautifully executed. Cassie expected her also to receive some praise.

But instead, Miss Wrench called Emily over to her and scrutinised her from head to foot. 'Untidy uniform,' she announced at the end of this embarrassing exercise. 'Not up to standard. What's your name?'

'Emily Pickering, Miss Wrench,' Emily replied, with a curtsey.

'I'll make a note of this, Emily,' Miss Wrench continued. 'Your turn-out in class must be improved.'

Cassie's anger with the Principal intensified. Couldn't she at least have given Emily credit for her lovely pas de chats?

By the end of the lesson, Cassie had made up her mind to confront Emily and apologise. But she couldn't find her in the changing rooms.

'Seen Emily?' she asked the others.

'I think I saw her heading for the loos,' replied Jane.

Cassie found her sobbing in one of the cubicles. She put her arm round her and rested her head on her friend's shoulder. She could easily have burst out crying herself.

'I'm ever so sorry, Em,' she whispered, 'for the nasty things I said.'

When the girls had made friends, and Emily had calmed down, they found Becky and went off to the dining hall for their supper. Over shepherd's pie, Emily told them she had been thinking hard.

'I've made up my mind now,' she said. 'I'm going to leave Redwood.'

Cassie and Becky were stunned. 'Not just because the silly old Wrench embarrassed you?' asked Becky.

'No, no. It's just no use. I can see that now. I'll never afford all the new ballet uniform and shoes we keep needing. I'm just going to keep getting into trouble. I might as well give up now.'

'Oh Emily, please don't leave,' pleaded Cassie. 'Why don't you go and talk to Miss Eiseldown before you make up your mind. She's *so* sympathetic.'

'No, Cassie, I've made my decision.'

'But do you think you don't want to be a dancer any more, is that it?'

'I want to dance more than almost anything else in the world.'

Cassie noticed the 'almost' and sensed she was thinking about her father.

'Oh *please* go and see Miss Eiseldown. You could tell her about your mum and dad . . .' Cassie could have kicked herself. Why did she always say the wrong thing?

Emily's eyes flashed, but she didn't speak. Cassie could see she was just too proud to go to a teacher with her problems. She sighed heavily.

'Look, Emily, just promise us you won't do anything about leaving till the end of term. It's not long now till Christmas. At least wait till then. Something might turn up.'

Emily agreed to this, and before she could change her mind, Cassie whisked her off to her bedroom, telling her on the way about the exciting events of Hallowe'en.

'So you think it was Mr Flint coming out of the cottage?' asked Emily, settling down on Becky's bed.

'Yes it was definitely him,' said Cassie. 'I still can't think where I've seen that man before. He gives me a funny feeling.'

'You and your funny feelings,' scoffed Becky, unwrapping a chocolate digestive bar. 'He seems a jolly old gentleman to me.'

'No, I know what Cassie means,' agreed Emily. 'He's a bit, you know, creepy.'

'Well let's keep an eye on things,' suggested Cassie. 'The weather's not much good for gardening, but we could offer to do some cleaning for her.'

'Right,' said Becky. 'We can't go tomorrow lunch-time, because of my cello lesson. It'll have to be Thursday.'

The next morning there was no Madame to greet them. Miss Oakland was taking over the class again. After their usual barre practice – there were no floor exercises any longer – the young teacher brought them into the centre. Cassie noticed her eyes lingering on Emily's outfit. Cassie had persuaded Emily, fortunately, to borrow one of her leotards, and so she looked quite smart.

Miss Oakland taught them a new adage sequence. When they had grasped the steps and run through it a few times, Miss Oakland asked the pianist to accompany them. Cassie recognised the tune. It was the slow movement from 'Winter'. Vivaldi's *The Four Seasons* was one of her favourite pieces of classical music. Her mum and dad had a tape of it at home and she often listened to it at bedtime.

At the end of the adage, Miss Oakland asked, 'Can anyone tell me what that piece of music was?'

Cassie put up her hand.

'Yes, Cassandra?'

' "Winter" from *The Four Seasons*, Miss Oakland.'

'Quite right. Well done.' The teacher smiled at her. Cassie felt pleased to have done something right for a change.

'Now girls, I'll let you into a little secret. We have decided what we're doing with the Juniors for the Christmas production. As the music suggests, we are taking the theme of winter. Of course, most of the solo parts will be taken by the older second year students, but you will be pleased to know that Miss Wrench has selected one of your group for a solo. A great honour, I may say, for a first year.'

There was a murmur of anticipation. *Please let it be me*, wished Cassie, knowing full well it couldn't possibly be.

'Amanda,' Miss Oakland said, beaming in her direction. 'You're to dance the part of Holly. Miss Wrench will be giving you coaching in the evenings after supper, while the others are learning their group dances.'

Only Amanda's eyes showed her pleasure at this news. Cassie looked away. She had known all along it would be Amanda. She dimly heard Miss Oakland telling the class that they would have a rehearsal that evening at seven o'clock sharp.

By the end of the class, they had worked so hard, that Cassie had shaken off her feeling of disappointment.

The girls spent a busy day together and after supper, had enough energy left to go to their rehearsal with enthusiasm. Cassie felt excited at the prospect of their first Redwood production. What made it even better was that Madame Larette was waiting in the studio for them, not Miss Oakland.

'Now, *mes chéries*,' Madame began, after their curtsey. 'Miss Oakland 'as shown you a drop of your dance, *n'est-ce pas*?'

The girls murmured their agreement.

'This one is the snowflake dance. You are all snowflakes. Light as air, graceful, beautiful!'

Madame called for the pianist to start and the lovely melody from 'Winter' accompanied the girls as they performed their slow adage.

'*Très bien!*' Madame cried at the end. 'Cassandra, could you go next door and tell the boys we are ready for them now, please.'

Cassie felt a little flustered, but also pleased, to be given this errand. She knocked on the door of the adjoining studio and the boys' ballet-master asked her to come in. After delivering her message, the boys followed her back to show Madame what they had been learning. Their dance, which went just before the girls', was meant to represent flurries of hail and sleet, and was accompanied by a much faster excerpt from 'Winter'. Cassie found it fascinating and exciting to watch them. She noticed again the tall boy, Matthew. He really was a most athletic dancer.

After the girls had followed on with their gentler dance, Madame started organising the children into smaller, mixed groups for further dances and explained they wouldn't be learning anything else tonight.

Cassie was placed in a group with Emily, Jane, Matthew and another quite tall boy called Paul. They were told they would be a group of birds who had stayed in Britain in the cold weather and who were desperately seeking food. This was to be in a later scene of the production.

The rehearsal finished half an hour before bedtime. As Cassie, Becky and Emily made their way back to their wing, they passed the practice room where Miss Wrench was coaching Amanda.

Another pang of jealousy shot through Cassie. She had to force herself to chat to the others and she felt relieved when she was in bed, ready for lights out. Amanda still wasn't back.

'Anything the matter, Cassie?' Becky asked from her bed. 'You've gone a bit quiet.'

'Oh nothing,' said Cassie. 'Well, that's not quite true. I'm a bit fed up about Amanda getting the only solo. Why couldn't they have given us a few more solos? It wouldn't have hurt them.'

'There would never be enough solos to go round,' said Becky wisely. 'Someone always has to be disappointed, it strikes me.' She shrugged and smiled. 'It's just better not to bother.'

Amanda came in at that moment and the friends fell silent. Cassie tried hard to be pleasant to her, and asked her questions about her solo. But she found it hard, especially as Amanda wasn't at all friendly.

Lying in the dark, Cassie went over in her mind the occasion only a few months before when she had danced Alice in her old dancing school's production of *Alice in Wonderland*. It had been a lovely end to her time with Miss Lakeley. She had danced in every scene, and had felt in every way the star of the show. She remembered the applause in the town hall, as she had taken her curtain-call and been presented with a lovely bouquet of flowers, just like a real ballerina.

She wondered if such a time would ever come again, or was she destined only for the corps de ballet? Not to be a dancer at all was unthinkable. She fell asleep with the noise of applause in her ears.

9

A Missed Lesson

Thursday brought heavy rain and high winds. In their Maths lesson, all the classroom lights were full on. Cassie wondered if it would be too wet for the girls to go across to Mrs Allingham's that lunch hour. She hoped they would be able to go, partly to try and find out a little more about Mr Flint and partly to keep Emily off the subject of leaving Redwood.

When lunch break came, the other two weren't very keen on braving the storm. But Cassie badgered them until they gave in. They muffled themselves in cagoules and wellingtons and trudged across the grounds against the howling wind.

'Whose bright idea was this?' shouted Becky.

'Cassie's, of course!' yelled Emily.

'Oh, stop moaning, you two. Think of that cup of hot chocolate!'

Mrs Allingham was surprised to see them in such weather, but glad all the same. She ushered them in and took their wet raincoats.

'Go and make yourselves comfortable,' she said. 'I'll make you a nice cup of chocolate.'

'Thank you,' said Cassie. 'But we'll stay in the kitchen with you. We've come to work.'

'Well, that's extremely kind. I wouldn't say no to a little help with my baking. I was just about to make some scones for my visitor.'

Emily and Cassie exchanged glances.

'We'd love to help you,' said Becky with a grin. 'Why don't you sit down and tell us what to do?'

The girls set to work with enthusiasm. Between instructions, Mrs Allingham seemed rather worried about something. Cassie was frightened of saying the wrong thing, but in the end couldn't stop herself from asking the old lady if there was anything the matter.

'Well, bless you dear. I *do* have something on my mind. I've had a number of large bills to pay recently and it's left me a bit short.'

Three worried faces looked up at her. She laughed.

'Nothing to get too anxious about. It'll sort itself

out. I'll just have to be a bit careful for a while. There, I feel quite better now I've told you all about it.'

Mrs Allingham certainly did seem more light-hearted after telling them. Cassie couldn't help thinking it must be easy to let little worries grow into big ones, if you lived on your own. She was curious to know who Mrs Allingham's visitor was, but knew it was rude to ask outright. Her opportunity came when Emily was taking the delicious-smelling batch of scones out of the Aga.

'They look lovely,' the old lady said. 'He's going to have a treat, isn't he?'

'Who?' asked Cassie innocently.

'Mr Flint. He's coming round this afternoon.' She consulted the kitchen clock – a large mahogany ship's clock hanging over the door. 'He won't be very long now.'

Cassie was filled with a very strong desire to stay there until Mr Flint came. She didn't trust him at all. A wicked idea came into her head.

'Would you mind if we stayed with you for another hour or so?'

'Now that *would* be nice. But what about your afternoon lessons, Cassandra?'

Emily and Becky were both looking mystified, but luckily Mrs Allingham was only paying attention to Cassie.

'Oh, our first lesson has been cancelled. The

Geography teacher is ill and we were told just to use it as a study period.'

As the fib came tumbling out, Cassie went very red and didn't dare look at her friends. Instead, she rushed over to the sink and started washing up the cooking utensils. She knew she had put Emily and Becky in a very awkward position but guessed, rightly, that they wouldn't contradict her story.

Thus the three girls were happily eating scones when Mr Flint arrived. He looked a little taken aback to see them.

'And how are our little ballerinas today?' he asked with a forced smile. Cassie was intrigued by a parcel wrapped in brown paper, which he had brought under his arm. He made a move to put it down at the side of his chair, but Mrs Allingham stopped him.

'Oh, do let me see my paintings,' she said excitedly. 'Would you mind unwrapping them for me?'

'No, of course not, June. Here we are.'

He took out two paintings which Cassie recognised from Mrs Allingham's sitting-room.

'Oh, you've made a beautiful job of these,' said Mrs Allingham. 'The colours are so much brighter now. Especially the poppies.'

Cassie looked at the smaller of the two pictures. A boy and girl, dressed in Victorian clothing, were playing in a field, aflame with poppies.

'So glad, so glad,' Mr Flint simpered. He was

smiling still, but his eyes were narrow. 'It's taken a lot of work, to restore them properly. Oh yes indeed. A lot of work.'

As he spoke, Cassie had an uncomfortable feeling in her stomach, but Mrs Allingham and her visitor settled down for a cosy chat about restoring paintings, and so Cassie thought nothing more could be gained by staying any longer.

Emily and Becky were relieved to be going back to school, and, once out of earshot of the cottage, gave Cassie the telling-off she deserved.

'You really dumped us in it,' Becky complained. 'We couldn't do anything but go along with your story.'

'Look, I'm sorry,' said Cassie. 'It was wicked of me, I know, but I just wanted to be there when Mr Flint came.'

'I think we should stop worrying about Mr Flint,' said Emily. 'He did seem nice today. And nothing awful happened, did it?'

'No,' said Cassie, 'but you never know, if we hadn't been there . . .'

'You're being daft, Cassie. And now we're going to get into heaps of trouble.'

'We'll be in time for English. Mr Dale might not have missed us in Geography.'

'Well, cross your fingers,' said Becky. 'We'll soon find out.'

They found out even sooner than they expected. The rain had abated and as they neared the back entrance of school, they could see Mr Dale waiting for them.

'Oh no,' groaned Becky. 'Do you see what I see?'

Approaching Mr Dale, Cassie saw Amanda retreating through the door into school.

'I bet she's had something to do with it,' she whispered.

'Have you girls deliberately missed my lesson?' Mr Dale asked.

'Well, not exactly,' said Cassie. 'We, er, just didn't notice the time.'

'That's no excuse, Cassandra, and you know it. You'll find yourselves speaking to Miss Wrench—'

The girls held their breath.

'—if this ever happens again!'

'Sorry, Mr Dale,' Cassie said. She was genuinely sorry that she had got her friends into trouble.

'I shall put the three of you on litter duty. That's every lunch-break for the next three days.'

Fortunately for Cassie, her friends transferred their anger from her to Amanda.

'He probably wouldn't have noticed, if *she* hadn't told on us,' said Emily at supper-time.

'Yes, you know what Mr Dale's like,' agreed Becky. 'In a dream most of the time.'

'I'm so cross with her, I'm going to stop speaking to her,' said Emily. 'Perhaps it'll make her think twice before she tells tales again.'

Cassie and Becky agreed, though it was harder for them to carry it out, as they shared a room with

110

her. Amanda soon got the message however. The next morning, she was up first and had left the bedroom before Cassie and Becky had started dressing.

'She doesn't seem very bothered,' Becky commented, as she helped Cassie with her plaits. 'Shall we keep it going a bit longer?'

'Yes,' said Cassie. 'I don't have anything to say to her anyway.'

The girls were pleased to see the weather was a lot brighter for their litter-picking. After morning ballet class with Miss Oakland, in which the teacher reprimanded Emily once more for the shabby state of her shoes, the girls went to their English lesson, feeling glum.

Cassie tried to settle her mind to writing a story on the title 'Escape!', but just kept thinking how awful it would be if Emily really did have to leave. She knew by looking at her that Emily was having the same thoughts. Eventually, though, she started her story. She had written three sides and was beginning to enjoy letting her imagination rip, when a thought flashed through her mind – she had no idea where it came from. Instantly she stopped writing and put down her pen.

Mr Flint! It was coming back to her now. The day her mother had picked her up from school and taken her into the city for her leotards. That's where she had seen him before! In the antique shop where her mum had gone to ask about a scrubbed-top table. So Mr Flint was an antiques dealer!

Feverishly scribbling a note about what she'd remembered, she passed it to Emily, who read it, nodded, and passed it to Becky. Cassie could see Amanda watching them like a hawk.

I bet she's dying to know what's in the note, Cassie thought.

Becky had noticed too and made a great show of screwing the scrap of paper into a tiny ball, popping it into her mouth and swallowing it. She grinned cheekily at Amanda.

Cassie was disappointed later, to find that her friends couldn't see the significance of her discovery.

'Mrs Allingham almost certainly knows already,' said Becky. 'I mean she told us she met him at an auction.'

'*And* he restored those pictures for her,' said Emily. 'She must know he's in that line of business.'

'Yes!' Cassie said. 'I know that, but . . .'

All through litter duty, Cassie kept turning it over in her mind.

'What if she *doesn't* know,' she blurted out at last. 'And he's wheedled his way into her cottage.'

'You're *so* suspicious, Cassie!' cried Becky.

'Well,' said Cassie. 'She's got a lot of antiques and stuff. Some of it could be valuable.'

'I expect he's perfectly honest,' said Becky, 'and has told her he's a dealer.'

'Let's ask her!' cried Cassie. 'It would only take a

minute or two to run over. We've already picked up loads of litter!'

The other two were dubious, but the force of Cassie's enthusiasm won them over and a few minutes later they found themselves panting on Mrs Allingham's doorstep.

'Oh girls, what a nice surprise!' Mrs Allingham said as she answered their knock. Cassie quickly explained they hadn't much time, but had a question to ask her.

'The thing is, Mrs Allingham, we were wondering about Mr Flint. You see, I think I've seen him before in an antiques shop.'

'Very likely, dear. He's passionately fond of collecting them. As I am!'

'No, no, I mean he was the *owner* of the shop, in Birmingham. I just wondered if you knew about it.'

'I think you're mistaken, Cassandra. Mr Flint has no shop. He's an artist,' she said proudly, 'and restores pictures as a sideline. You saw the two he did for me, didn't you?'

'Yes, they look great,' said Becky.

'Poor Mr Flint had such a time of it. Quite a difficult job, he told me. Took him hours and hours. Quite unexpected too. He was so reluctant to charge me the full amount for his work, but I told him friends must honour their obligations even more than strangers.'

Emily and Becky were looking rather blankly at

113

the old lady, but Cassie was following the drift of this all too well.

'So it was a large bill, was it?' she asked sharply.

'Yes dear. But *you* know Mr Flint. Rather than put me to any embarrassment – because I'd told him of my little troubles, of course – he kindly offered to take the smaller picture instead of payment.'

Cassie gasped. 'But that's the lovely poppy-field one, isn't it?'

'Yes. I said I'd let him know next week, but really I haven't any choice. I can't afford to pay him.'

'Why don't you let him have the other picture,' suggested Becky. 'It's not so pretty.'

'I know, dear, but Mr Flint wouldn't hear of taking the larger one. He said it was the more valuable of the two. But really, I'm not so fond at all of that one.'

'When's he coming back for it?' asked Cassie.

'Not until next week.'

She looked so wistful at that moment that Cassie determined then and there to save Mrs Allingham from the dreadful Mr Flint. But how was she to do it?

10

A Saturday Outing

'I still don't know what you're making all the fuss about,' complained Becky that evening. She and Cassie were alone in their bedroom. Amanda had gone to Miss Wrench, for more coaching on her solo.

'Oh, don't you see,' said an exasperated Cassie. 'Old Flinty-face has got Mrs Allingham just where he wants her!'

'I thought it was kind of him to let her give him the painting instead of money.'

'But, Becky, what if that painting turns out to be worth a *lot* of money. You notice he wasn't at all keen to have the other one.'

'He explained the reason for that – it's the more valuable of the two,' Becky argued.

'And my cat's sky blue pink with spots on!' cried Cassie. 'Come on, let's go and ask Emily round. Might stop her brooding.'

Emily certainly didn't look happy when she emerged from her room. Cassie went out of her way to interest her in the debate about Mr Flint and asked her what she thought.

'There's too many ifs and buts at the moment,' said Emily. 'I don't know what to think really, but I do feel a bit suspicious of him.'

'We need to do a bit more detective work,' said Cassie, with some excitement in her voice. 'For a start, I suppose I should find out for sure that Mr Flint *is* an antiques dealer.'

'Yes,' agreed Becky. 'I mean, he might just have been helping out in the shop the day you saw him through the window.'

'We could try phoning the shop,' suggested Emily.

'Brilliant!' cried Cassie. 'Why didn't I think of that?'

Emily ran off to find the telephone directory, and the girls pored over the lines of names beginning with F, but not one Flint was listed.

'He probably lives outside the area,' said Becky.

'Or it's not his real name!' said Cassie.

'Oh, stop being so melodramatic!'

'No, wait,' said Cassie. 'There is another explanation. The shop has a different name. If only I can remember.' She thought hard for a few moments. 'I think I've got it. The Treasure Box. Yes, I'm sure that was it.'

This time their search was more fruitful. They were allowed to phone their parents on Fridays and Tuesdays, and so, after the three girls had each phoned their mums, Cassie dialled the shop number.

A familiar voice came on the other end of the line.

'Treasure Box.'

Cassie hadn't thought about what she was going to say if Mr Flint answered, but her natural dramatic talent helped her out. She assumed the voice of an elderly woman and asked,

'Erm, who am I speaking to?'

'Flint here. Can I help you?'

'Where's Terry?' she croaked.

'Terry? There's no Terry here,' answered Mr Flint, struggling to conceal his impatience. 'Are you sure you have the right number, Madam? This is an antiques shop and I am its proprietor. I have no assistant called Terry, I assure you.'

'Oh, so sorry,' warbled Cassie. 'Goodbye.'

Emily and Becky had been aching to laugh all through the conversation, and now they let themselves go wholeheartedly. Looking up, Cassie nudged them both in the ribs. Miss Oakland was approaching down the corridor. They managed to keep straight faces long enough to curtsey to her and mumble, 'Good evening.'

After she had gone past, they scurried back to the bedroom, where Cassie told her friends what Mr Flint had said. Becky looked impressed.

'Well, you're right so far,' she said.

'Next thing we have to find out is the true value of that painting,' said Cassie.

'Wouldn't it be funny if it was worth a fortune!' cried Emily.

'Mrs Allingham would know if it was. She'd have it insured and everything,' said Becky.

'She might not, though,' said Cassie. 'Haven't you ever watched that antiques programme on telly? There's always some old painting someone's had hanging in the garden shed which turns out to be worth thousands!'

Further conversation had to be postponed until the morning, as Amanda returned to the bedroom, and it was almost time for lights out anyway. The girls still weren't speaking to her, but Amanda showed no sign of letting it bother her in the slightest.

Cassie fell asleep quickly, but had a strange dream about three Mr Flints who were picking all the poppies out of Mrs Allingham's painting.

The next day was Saturday. The girls spent all morning, along with the rest of the Junior school, in rehearsals for their Christmas production. Cassie and Emily's group – the bird group as they were nicknamed – were coached by Madame Larette. She taught them the steps of their dance. Cassie found it strange at first, working so closely with the boys, although as there were three girls and only two boys, there was no direct pair-dancing. Even so, there were a couple of times when she had to link hands with Matthew and at the very end, he went down on one knee and she had to rest her hand on his other knee, while balancing in a low arabesque. But by the end of the class, it seemed the easiest, most natural thing in the world to be dancing with boys.

The girls' lunch hour of course was again devoted to picking up litter, though they found far less than the day before. They got back to their rooms in good time to change out of their tracksuits, into their school uniform and blazers, for Saturday afternoon gave them the opportunity to go into the nearest village, which was really a suburb of the city. Before this came the weekly ritual of handing out pocket-money. Miss Eiseldown gave them each £1 and said, 'Don't spend it all at once!'

There wasn't a great variety of shops in the village, but most of the children were only interested in buying sweets and comics. Cassie and Becky were no exception, but Emily had only come along for the outing – she could not afford to spend any of her precious pocket-money. Becky insisted on buying her a chocolate bar, and, perhaps because she was feeling so down, for once Emily accepted it.

When they got back to school, Cassie and Becky had to do some music practice, as they hadn't had a chance all week. But all day, Cassie had been thinking about Mr Flint and the painting, and now she couldn't concentrate on her music. Cassie put her violin back in its case and suggested they go back to Mrs Allingham's.

'What, again?' Becky exclaimed.

'It's important,' said Cassie. 'Old Flinty-face is going to get his hands on that picture next week. I want to look at it again.'

They called for Emily on their way and found her miserably counting her savings on her bed.

'If only I were at home at weekends more,' she complained, during their walk across the lawns. 'I could earn a bit extra.'

'You've got a weekend at home coming up soon,' said Cassie.

'I know, but I owe pounds and pounds for the shoes and tights I've already had from the stock-room – much more than I've saved. *And* I need a new pair of character shoes.'

'Don't worry, Em,' said Becky kindly. 'We'll find a way.'

'Yes, I must stop it,' sighed Emily. 'I *have* found a solution after all. After Christmas I can relax.'

Cassie and Becky exchanged glances but said no more.

When they reached the cottage, Cassie made a mental note of the details of the painting. The subject matter was already etched on her brain, but now she noted the artist's signature and the date, while Mrs Allingham chatted to Becky and Emily.

'What's your Christmas production going to be this year?' she was asking.

'It's called *Winter Wonderland*,' answered Becky. 'And it's set to Vivaldi's "Winter" concerto.'

'That sounds lovely. I shall phone Miss Wrench and ask her to save me a ticket.'

The girls stayed for half an hour before heading back to school. After supper, Emily wanted to watch some programmes on TV so she stopped off at the common room with her room-mates, Miranda and Jane. Cassie and Becky decided to read in their rooms: Cassie was looking forward to starting the epic *Lord of the Rings* and Becky had a couple of books about bats she wanted to delve into.

They found they had the bedroom to themselves.

'What *are* we going to do about Emily?' sighed Cassie.

'I don't know,' said Becky. 'But I think she really has made up her mind to leave.'

'It would be so sad,' said Cassie. 'She so loves ballet, and she's such a promising dancer. Oh, I do wish we could do something.'

'So do I,' said Becky. 'All we can do at the moment is keep her mind off it, and hope something turns up.'

'At least this Mrs Allingham thing has given her something else to think about.'

'How are we going to find out about the painting?' Becky asked.

'I'm not sure. I remember Amanda saying her father's an artist, so perhaps she'd know.'

'Trouble is, we're not speaking to her.'

'Well, we've got to start again *some* time,' said Cassie, grinning. 'Anyway, I feel a bit mean now.'

'Yes, so do I,' said Becky, looking relieved.

As if on cue, Amanda sauntered in through the door. She wore a sort of mask of indifference on her face and Cassie suddenly guessed that she was probably quite hurt underneath this front.

'Hello, Amanda,' she said, in a friendly tone.

Amanda was caught off-guard and Cassie saw surprise flash across her face. It was just as quickly concealed.

'I suppose that means you want something,' she drawled.

'Well, yes, in a way. We need your advice really. But we're sorry too about not speaking to you.'

'Well at least I've had a bit of peace,' said Amanda. 'What's the advice you want from me?'

'Did you say your dad's an artist?'

'Yes – portraits, landscapes, the lot.'

'Well, how would you go about getting a painting valued?'

'A modern one, do you mean?'

'No, an old one,' said Becky.

'That's easy,' said Amanda loftily. 'Take it to an auction house of course – Sotheby's for instance. They have valuers there.'

'Thanks Amanda,' said Cassie. 'You've been a great help.'

'Whose picture is it anyway?'

'Oh, just a friend's,' said Cassie airily. 'No one you know.'

She could see Amanda was torn between wanting to ask some more questions and wanting to keep aloof. Turning away from her, Cassie opened her book and settled into a delicious read.

11

A Budding Actress

Cassie was very glad of such an exciting book to read over the weekend. Without it, she guessed the time would have dragged, as their investigations into the poppy picture couldn't resume until Monday.

When Monday came, there was still an obstacle. They had found a telephone number for Sotheby's but phone calls were only allowed on Tuesday and Friday evenings, when the auction house would be closed.

Cassie, however, wasn't one to give up. Her friends suggested they wait until the coming weekend, when they would all be going home, but she was horrified by the suggestion.

'It'll be far too late then. Flinty-face will have the painting. In fact he might even have *sold* it by the weekend.'

'You're so sure it's valuable, aren't you?' said Becky. 'It'll probably turn out to be worth about ten pounds.'

'What can we do, then, Cassie?' asked Emily. 'We're not allowed to go into the village, and it's too risky trying to use a school phone in the daytime, when there are masses of teachers about.'

'There's only one solution!' cried Cassie. 'We'll have to phone from Mrs Allingham's!'

'But we can't tell her why.'

'No, I'll have to say it's a private call, and not tell her the reason.'

'She's sure to be suspicious.'

'Well, if it goes as I think it will, we won't have to keep her in the dark for long.'

Cassie didn't much enjoy her ballet class that morning. She couldn't keep her mind on her dancing for more than two minutes together. This wasn't too disastrous during the routine barre and centre exercises, because she could do these on automatic pilot. But when Miss Oakland began to teach the girls a new enchaînement of steps, it quickly became obvious to the teacher that Cassie wasn't concentrating.

She stopped the pianist and turned on Cassie.

'Why is it, Cassandra, that every single girl in this class, *except* you, has picked up the new steps? Is it because you are more stupid than everyone else, or what?'

Miss Oakland waited for an answer, hands on hips, a nerve in her cheek twitching irritably.

'I'm sorry, Miss Oakland,' Cassie stammered. 'I can't seem to keep my mind on what I am doing.'

'That is very obvious. I'm afraid you're no good to me in your present condition, or to anyone else for that matter.'

'No, Miss Oakland.'

'Slapdash efforts will not be tolerated at Redwood. I thought you had realised that by now. You are dismissed from the remainer of class. And please *think* about what I have said.'

'Yes, Miss Oakland.'

It was a full half an hour before the end of class. Most first years would have cried at this disgrace, but not Cassie. She felt her eyes prickling, but told herself sternly not to take any notice. She walked out with her chin held high and spent the half hour in the changing room, mulling over what she would say to the valuer at Sotheby's.

Her friends crowded round her when they had finished, full of sympathy. Cassie just grinned at them, bright-eyed, but with a flush to her cheek which gave away what she was really feeling.

Miss Eiseldown's Maths lesson, which followed,

was torture to Cassie. She found Maths a difficult subject at the best of times. Luckily, Becky, who was sitting beside her, could see what she was going through, and made sure Cassie could read her own working-out of the decimal problems they had been set.

At last it was lunch-time. The girls gobbled down pizza and chips, not waiting for pudding, which Becky found very hard, and ran all the way to Mrs Allingham's. Cassie had brought her purse with her, in order to pay for the call.

They knocked and waited, but there was no response.

'She's out,' said Becky.

'Well, I can see that,' said Cassie irritably.

'Hey, you don't think we're too late?' cried Emily. 'She might be meeting Mr Flint somewhere for lunch, and have taken the painting.'

Cassie groaned. This was too much to bear. As they began to walk away, a cheerful voice hailed them from the side path.

'Hello, girls. Were you looking for me?' called Mrs Allingham, her knobbly hands clutching two shopping bags. 'I've just been out for a few groceries.'

Cassie felt so relieved she could have kissed her. When they were all inside, and had helped Mrs Allingham to unpack her bags, Cassie plucked up courage to ask her an important question.

'Are you expecting Mr Flint this afternoon?'

'No, dear. He *is* coming tomorrow though, for lunch.'

Cassie's stomach gave a lurch. Everything now hung on the phone call she must make to Sotheby's. Just supposing there was no valuer available to speak to her. What then? She cast the thought aside and plunged into asking Mrs Allingham if she could possibly use the telephone.

'Yes, of course you may, Cassandra. It's in the hall, so I'm afraid you won't be very comfortable.'

Cassie laughed nervously. 'I won't stay on very long anyway. I just need to check something out – urgently.'

Mrs Allingham, too polite to ask any more, led her into the hall. Becky followed her, but Emily thought she'd better stay in the kitchen and talk to Mrs Allingham, so she wouldn't overhear any of Cassie's conversation.

'You're sure you want to go through with this?' whispered Becky. 'I mean, do you know what to say?'

'Of course – I've worked it all out,' said Cassie. Becky admired her friend's assurance. As she began speaking to the receptionist at the auction house, Becky had a shock. Cassie had assumed a quite grown-up, plum-in-the-mouth sort of voice. Becky wondered whatever Mrs Allingham would make of it, if she could hear.

'Is it possible to be given a rough valuation of a painting over the phone?'

Cassie was asked to hold the line. 'Hope they don't take ages to find the valuer,' she whispered. 'Or I'll have to pay a lot for the call.'

Becky giggled at the sudden change of voice.

A few moments later, Cassie took up the posh voice once more. The valuer was on the other end of the line, asking for details of the painting.

'And the signature says Myles Birket Foster,' she concluded.

'And you say there are two figures – children?'

'Yes, a girl with very blonde hair, and a younger boy. They're picking the poppies.'

'Mmm,' said the valuer. 'Sounds very promising. You're thinking of selling, I take it?'

'Er . . .' This threw Cassie into momentary confusion. 'You see, my good man—'

Becky was holding her sides, dying to laugh out loud.

'—it belongs to a friend of mine,' Cassie continued. 'She may want to sell it, depending on the value.'

'Yes I see. Of course, I would need to see it, to verify that it's genuine. But you can tell your friend it could fetch over thirty thousand pounds.'

Cassie's mouth fell open. 'WOW!' she shrieked in a very un-grown-up manner. There was a puzzled silence on the other end of the line, as she and Becky both collapsed in giggles. When she was composed enough to speak, she dispensed with the fake voice and apologised.

'Is this some sort of practical joke?' asked the mystified valuer.

'No, no, it's quite serious,' Cassie said earnestly. 'My friend really might want to sell her painting, but she's old and doesn't get out much.'

'I see,' said the valuer, still trying to weigh up whether the young voice was to be trusted.

'The thing is,' Cassie blurted out, 'she's probably going to give it away tomorrow to a friend, who she thinks is an artist, but really he's an antiques dealer. He's sort of tricked her into it and I thought I'd better find out if it was valuable before she made a terrible mistake and she could really do with the money and we don't want to see her being tricked, because she's such a nice old lady and . . .'

'Stop!' cried the valuer, laughing. 'I think I've got the general idea. And I agree, you do need to act quickly. Do you think your friend would mind if I came to her house to confirm that the picture's genuine? At least then she'd have accurate information on which to make a decision.'

Overjoyed at the offer, Cassie quickly gave the young man Mrs Allingham's name and address.

'Could you come at about half past one, do you think?'

'Yes, that would be fine. I look forward to meeting your Mrs Allingham and, if I may say so, such an accomplished young actress as yourself.'

Cassie, flustered by his words, and not knowing whether they were complimentary or not, rushed her goodbye and replaced the receiver as though it were hot.

As they'd expected, Mrs Allingham was surprised at the information that Mr Flint really was an antiques dealer, but soon found a charitable explanation.

'Well, I wonder why he pretended,' she mused. 'Perhaps he thought it wasn't an interesting enough occupation, silly man. I'd have liked him just as much, even if he wasn't an artist.'

'That's not the worst of it, I'm afraid, Mrs Allingham,' Cassie went on, as gently as she could.

'Perhaps you should sit down,' broke in Becky, anxiously. She couldn't bear for anyone, whether animal or human, to be hurt.

Mrs Allingham sat down in her rocking chair. She still wasn't taking the conversation terribly seriously.

'What was all that shrieking and giggling coming from the hall?' she asked, her eyes twinkling. 'You haven't got a boyfriend, have you, Cassandra?'

'No, Mrs Allingham, nothing like that. The phone call was for you really.'

'Me, dear?'

'About your poppy picture. I phoned Sotheby's and, well, if it's genuine they said it's worth over thirty thousand pounds.'

'Well!' was all the old lady could manage, with an out-blowing of breath. She looked absolutely thunderstruck.

It was news to Emily and Becky too, of course, and they looked flabbergasted as well. Cassie began to enjoy herself. Centre stage was her favourite position.

'And he kindly offered to come and look at it tomorrow at one thirty for you, to make sure it's not a fake. But I don't think it is, for a moment.'

'Thirty thousand!' said Becky, whistling in admiration. 'Think how many boxes of chocolates you could buy with that!'

'Or how many pairs of ballet shoes,' said Emily, which immediately made Becky feel desperately guilty.

'Whatever will Mr Flint say when I tell him?' Mrs Allingham cried, laughing. 'I'll be able to pay his bill after all, and all my other ones!'

Cassie hadn't the heart to tell her she was jolly sure Mr Flint knew already. At least Mrs Allingham wouldn't be parting with the picture tomorrow. That was the important thing for now.

The next day, Cassie redeemed herself a little with Miss Oakland. Now her investigations were over, her mind was far more settled, and she made an extra effort to do her best work in ballet class. After lunch, she, Becky and Emily made haste to get to the cottage, hoping to arrive before Mr Flint.

When they got there, Mrs Allingham was just letting him in. This meant that the girls had the satisfaction of watching Mr Flint's face turn a shade of grey when Mrs Allingham told him her 'good news'. They were taken aback, however, by the way the conversation went on.

'Did you speak to Sotheby's yourself, June?' he asked, after his first obvious shock.

'No, Cassandra here took it upon herself. She must have an eye for quality, mustn't she?'

Mr Flint gave Cassie a look which made her feel very small. 'Well, I'm afraid I'll have to disappoint you, June. It's not genuine, you see. Just an imitation. A *good* imitation, I'll admit. Yes, I looked into it when I restored it for you. I'm so sorry.'

Cassie looked helplessly at Emily and Becky, who, she could see at a glance, were being taken in again by the devious Mr Flint. Mrs Allingham sat down heavily on the sofa, near to tears.

'What a crying shame!' she said. 'I thought all my problems were over.'

'Never mind,' said Emily, with great sympathy for her distress. 'It still might have some value.'

She put her arm comfortingly around the old lady's shoulder. Becky was practically in tears and didn't trust herself to speak.

Cassie thought fast. The valuer would be here soon. That was an ace up her sleeve that Flinty-face didn't know about. Delay was essential, and also she longed to trip him up in his own web of lies.

'Perhaps it's all for the best,' she said suddenly. Becky looked at her as though she'd gone mad. 'You see, Mr Flint, this is Mrs Allingham's favourite painting. She wouldn't have said anything to you, but now we know it's a fake, she could keep it. You could take the bigger one, which would be a better payment to you for your work.'

'No, no,' blustered Mr Flint. 'I wouldn't *dream* of depriving you of that one, June. It's worth *much* more.'

'Well, I don't mind that. Cassie's right, you know. I'd much rather keep my poppies.'

'No,' Mr Flint repeated. 'I insist I have the smaller one.' He was beginning to sound impatient.

Mrs Allingham went quiet, looking hard at Mr Flint. Cassie could see the truth was beginning to dawn on her at long last. In the uncomfortable silence, there came a knock at the door. Cassie breathed a huge sigh of relief.

'That'll be the man from Sotheby's,' said Mrs Allingham. 'If you'll excuse me one moment . . .'

'Sotheby's?' said Mr Flint. His eyes began to dart from side to side. He moved rapidly towards the kitchen.

'Must be going, girls,' he mumbled over his shoulder. 'Tell Mrs Allingham I let myself out.'

'Well, he didn't put up much of a fight, did he?' said Cassie, with a giggle.

Strangely Mrs Allingham didn't really seem all that surprised to find that her friend had slipped out through the back door. The young man from Sotheby's was extremely nice and gave Cassie a big wink when she was introduced to him.

'Oh, our budding actress. Pleased to meet you.'

Cassie turned very red.

'Now, let's have a look at your painting.'

The girls and Mrs Allingham stood nervously, while he took down the painting and studied it, back and front.

'Yes, there's no doubt in my mind. It's a genuine Myles Birket Foster, all right.'

'Oh, I'm so glad!' said Mrs Allingham, clapping her arthritic hands like a child.

'Now, I've done a little research for you,' the valuer went on. 'We sold one of his with a similar composition five years ago. That had children in it too – it was called *Gathering Wild Roses.*'

'What price did it fetch?' asked Cassie excitedly.

'Thirty thousand eight hundred pounds. And, of course, that was then. You can expect to increase that quite a bit.'

'I can't really believe it,' said Mrs Allingham, looking rather dazed.

'It's a lot to take in, I know,' said the young man. 'But do you think you would like us to sell it for you?'

'Yes indeed, I would,' she said immediately. 'But mind it goes to a good home.'

The young man smiled.

'It's given me a lot of pleasure over the years, and it's going to provide me with a bit of comfort in my old age!' added Mrs Allingham.

When the valuer had gone with the painting, Mrs Allingham went rather quiet again. Cassie guessed she was thinking about Mr Flint.

'How silly I've been,' she said.

'You weren't to know,' said Emily. 'He took us in too. It was only Cassie who guessed the truth.'

'Well, how can I ever thank you, Cassandra, for saving me from being duped?'

'It's nothing,' said Cassie, embarrassed. 'But do you think you should tell the police?'

'Well, he hasn't actually committed any crime, has he?'

'No, but if you told them, perhaps they could just warn him. It might stop him doing the same to someone else.'

'Yes, I take your point. Yes, I'll certainly speak to them, Cassandra. And now, girls, have you still time for hot chocolate and biscuits?'

12

The Christmas Production

Cassie couldn't believe the last day of term had come round so quickly. The Redwood Juniors had spent the last few weeks rehearsing in every spare moment, their dancing teachers impressing upon them that their Christmas performance had to be of the highest standard. Cassie had made every effort to get back into Miss Oakland's good books, and had been squeezing in as much private practice as she could. Her hard work was beginning to pay off, she felt, although the teacher never gave her any praise. In rehearsals with Madame Larette, however, Cassie received strong encouragement and felt herself improving in leaps and bounds.

There had been little time for any recreation; the girls hadn't even managed to get across to Mrs Allingham's cottage since the eventful day when the valuer came.

Miss Wrench took a special assembly for the combined Junior and Senior departments. In such a small hall, this was a terrible crush, but there was a festive atmosphere when the elder three years added their deeper voices to the carol-singing. The Principal was in a light-hearted mood, but, after wishing them all a very happy Christmas, still managed to remind them to do their very best in their production that afternoon.

Instead of ballet class and morning lessons, the Juniors were allowed a disco in the hall. Miss Eiseldown had organised it for them, in her role as senior tutor of the Junior Department, and had even managed to obtain flashing coloured lights. Everyone was enjoying themselves thoroughly.

Everyone, that is, except Emily.

Cassie and Becky went across to the chairs at the back of the hall, where Emily was sitting alone.

'What's the matter, Em?' asked Cassie. 'Why won't you get up and dance with us?'

'I've got things on my mind,' said Emily.

'Come on,' said Becky brightly. 'You've got through this term all right. We thought you'd put all that nonsense about leaving behind you.'

'Well, you thought wrong. I told you I'd made up my mind weeks ago.'

'Oh, you can't mean it,' cried Cassie. 'We'd miss you so much.'

Emily looked down and Cassie could see she was close to tears. 'I've no choice,' she said sadly.

'Couldn't you explain the problem to Miss Wrench? I'm sure she'd find a way . . .'

Emily shook her head and Cassie knew it was no use continuing. This conversation cast a blight over the disco, the Christmas lunch and the preparations for the production in the early afternoon. Normally, Cassie would have revelled in putting on stage make-up and costume and waiting in the changing-room for curtain up. But she felt so unhappy that Emily was leaving, both for her friend and for herself, that she felt no pleasure in these activities at all.

It wasn't until she peeped round the curtain on stage and saw her mum, dad, Adam and Rachel sitting in the front row that she felt a tremor of excitement. She called Becky and Emily from the changing room, so they could have a peek. Becky couldn't see her parents, but Cassie spotted Amanda's father taking a seat just behind her own family. Emily's mum was pretty obvious, with three children in tow and a baby in arms. Cassie thought she looked awkward, but no wonder, really, with all those young children to keep quiet for the next couple of hours.

'What do you think you're doing here?' said a

sharp voice behind them. It was Miss Oakland. 'Go back into the changing rooms and please stay there!'

To make quite sure, she accompanied them. She inspected their make-up and snowflake costumes and, after adjusting Cassie's white crêpe-paper head-dress, moved on to another group of first years.

A few moments later, Becky's mother came bursting into the changing room, with a huge box of peppermint creams for her much-loved daughter.

'Oh hello, Mum,' said Becky, looking embarrassed.

'Oh darling, you do look sweet. Good enough to eat!' said Mrs Hastings, fussing over her. 'Is your eyeshadow quite the right shade, I wonder?'

'Yes, Mum. Miss Oakland's already given me the OK.'

'Oh, isn't it exciting? I'm so looking forward to the show. Let me just take a little piccy of you here, before you go on. And your friends too.'

Three glum faces stared back at the camera.

'Well, *smile*. There's no need to be nervous, you know. You'll be fine.'

Miss Oakland approached them. 'I think it's almost time for us to begin, Mrs er . . . ?'

'Hastings. I'm Rebecca's mother. I couldn't resist a little peek at her before the show begins.'

'Quite,' said Miss Oakland. 'Now, if you'll excuse us . . .'

Mrs Hastings, taking the hint at last, left the room. Despite the visit from her mother, and even the peppermint creams, Becky looked as miserable as ever.

'Whatever's the matter with you three?' sighed Miss Oakland. 'You look as if you were waiting for an injection. Don't forget to smile when you're dancing, will you?'

She ordered everyone to be quiet, while Madame Larette introduced the Juniors' ballet, *Winter Wonderland*. Miss Oakland ushered all the snowflakes into the wings of the theatre, from where they took up their starting positions. Before the lovely music began, Cassie had time to notice that Mrs Allingham was sitting next to Miss Wrench in the front row, not far from the Brown family. She fixed a smile upon her face as she began to dance and wondered to herself if clowns often felt unhappy underneath their painted happy faces.

Her sadness was forgotten, however, as she let the music and movement take her over. She felt part of the swirling white mass of bodies, when the boys joined them in the faster section, and ran back to the changing room in much better spirits. She had a very quick change, as the bird-group dance was next. She and Emily raced to get into their feathery costumes, while Becky helped them to do up their back fasteners and change their head-dresses. They spilled on to the stage on the opposite side from the boys and began their dance. Cassie was conscious that more eyes would be on her now, in a much smaller group, and tried her best to make her placing as neat as possible. There were a lot of jumping steps in the dance, and Cassie remembered what Madame had urged upon them about using a good plié, both to achieve elevation and to guarantee a soft landing.

'Birds don't land like elephants!' she had often repeated to them.

When she wasn't thinking about her own footwork, Cassie kept a close eye on Emily. She was afraid that her friend might stumble, or even forget some of the steps. But although she didn't smile once, Emily, with the true spirit of a dancer, got through to the end without a single mistake. In their final group, Cassie stretched her back leg as high as she possibly could in her arabesque and felt quite proud of herself. It wasn't the same as being Alice, when she was the centre of attention, but nonetheless, she had gained something from being part of a small group of dancers, each one contributing his or her own personality and strengths.

She peered out into the audience. It was too dark to see anyone's faces clearly. It was just a blur of whitish circles. The clapping continued as she and her friends ran offstage and returned to the dressing room.

Becky was part of the next scene – a group of carol-singers – and so the three friends weren't together again until after Becky returned to the changing room. At this point, Amanda was about to go off to dance her solo. Miss Wrench had provided her with a magnificent costume for her part as Holly. It was a brilliant green tutu, decorated with green sequins, and red berries. The head-dress was a wreath of imitation holly leaves and red flowers. Cassie knew that the deep colours of the costume would look stunning against all the white dresses of the snowflakes, which they would be wearing again for the finale.

'Ready, Amanda?' called Miss Oakland.

Amanda gave a little shiver and nodded. As she left the changing room, with calls of 'Good luck!' following her, Cassie imagined for an instant that it was she, not Amanda, going out to dance the solo, she, not Amanda, who would receive the applause. She shook herself and glanced up at Emily, whose unhappy face made her count her own blessings.

'Come on, Em,' she said, patting her shoulder. 'Enjoy the show. It'll be a good memory, whatever happens after.'

'Are you ready for the finale, girls?' called Miss Oakland.

The friends quickly dressed once more in their snowflake costumes and assembled in an orderly double line, ready to leave the dressing room. As they ran lightly on stage, Amanda was still curtseying to the audience. She had received tremendous applause. The other three soloists, from the second year, including one boy, joined her.

Now they weaved in and out of the gracefully-moving snowflakes, and the spinning hailstones; then the corps de ballet encircled the soloists, as if in adoration. Finally they all bowed low as Amanda and the second year boy rose on demi-pointe, arms raised to the ceiling, in triumph.

If only it were me, thought Cassie, *if only it were me.*

Then the lights went up and she could see Adam and Rachel grinning and waving to her. Her mum and dad and Mrs Allingham were clapping and smiling. Miss Wrench mounted the stage and made a short speech, thanking her staff and pupils for their efforts, and the parents for taking the trouble to come.

'And of course,' she went on, 'the other rather important reason that brings you here today, is to collect your children and take them home with you for the Christmas holidays. We hope no one is overlooked!'

There was general laughter.

'And that everyone has a restful and enjoyable Christmas.'

As Cassie took off her snowflake costume for the last time, she thought what a wonderful first term it had been. There were regrets of course, the chief one being Emily leaving, and others too, that had been caused by her own fault. Like everyone else, Cassie had a Record of Achievement to take home with her, which she had been given the chance to read and comment on. Her academic reports were all glowing, as was Mr Green's account of her progress in violin. But Miss Oakland, who had written the ballet section, mentioned 'difficulties with concentration', and in the general remarks about her behaviour, Miss Eiseldown had had to include her black mark and litter duty, saying that high spirits had led Cassandra into trouble on occasions.

Then again, when she remembered the wonderful news about Mrs Allingham's painting, and the unmasking of Mr Flint, a litter duty didn't seem so very important. She had such a lot to tell her parents, but, for the moment, she knew that she had to give Emily some support. As she pressed her way through the crowded dressing room, she bumped into Amanda's father.

'I'm looking for Amanda Renwick,' he said stiffly.

'Oh, she's over there!' said Cassie, pointing her out. She watched him approach his daughter. He didn't give her a hug or a kiss, but presented her rather formally with a small bouquet.

As Cassie passed them, she heard him say, 'You need more *expression*, Amanda. And your port-de-bras was too stiff.' Remembering the warm smiles and waves from her own family, Cassie instantly felt sorry for Amanda.

Emily was at this point moving around the dressing room, tearfully saying goodbye to the other girls. This somehow made her departure seem far more real, and Cassie felt a knot tightening in the pit of her stomach. How Emily must be feeling she couldn't begin to guess.

Just then, the door opened and a smiling Miss Wrench entered, followed by Mrs Allingham. Emily, who was receiving a farewell hug from Becky, looked up in surprise.

'Well done, everyone,' called Miss Wrench, as curtseys were bobbed all around her.

Mrs Allingham had moved across to her three helpers. She shooed them over to a quiet corner. Cassie could see that she was very excited.

'My poppies were sold last week at auction, for forty-three thousand pounds! What do you think of that?'

Despite her own unhappiness, Emily beamed. 'That's wonderful, Mrs Allingham! I'm so pleased for you.'

'Don't spend it all at once!' quipped Becky.

'No fear of that. It's too much for a simple soul like me, but I'll put what I don't need to good use. Charities and so on. For a start, a little thank you to three girls without whom it wouldn't have happened.'

She drew out of her handbag an envelope which she asked Becky to open for her.

'Tickets for the Birmingham Royal Ballet's *Swan Lake*!' said a delighted Becky.

'In the front row,' added Mrs Allingham.

As the girls thanked her, Miss Wrench joined their circle.

'I'd like to congratulate you girls on some very neat detective work. Mrs Allingham has told me all about what you have done for her this term.'

'Hear, hear,' said Mrs Allingham. 'Can we tell them about my bursary?'

'I don't see why not, though it won't be announced formally of course till next term.'

'Well, my dears,' said Mrs Allingham, bursting with pleasure. 'I'm setting up an annual bursary for promising but needy pupils in the school, to cover the cost of uniform, equipment, music lessons, school tours and holidays, all those extras which aren't covered by your grant.'

Emily's eyes showed a flicker of hope, but she hardly dared to look at either Miss Wrench or Mrs Allingham.

'I shall award the Allingham Bursary at my discretion,' said Miss Wrench, 'and I have already, on Mrs Allingham's recommendation, decided on the first recipient . . .'

Even before Miss Wrench said the words, 'Emily Pickering', Cassie knew that her friend's problems had been solved at a stroke. She grinned at Emily and threw her arms around her wildly, just as Becky did the same.

'Don't knock poor Emily over!' laughed Mrs Allingham. When Emily emerged smiling from the scrum she thanked her benefactor.

'You'll never know how much this means to me,' she said, with feeling.

'Would you like me to leave you a little longer with the girls, June?' asked Miss Wrench.

'Yes, that would be very nice.'

'Well, if you'll excuse me, I've lots of parents to shake hands with.'

As Miss Wrench swept out of the changing room, Cassie marvelled that she had actually been *thanked* by the Principal. It certainly made a welcome change.

'Now, what shall we do with Mrs Allingham?' said Cassie, her eyes sparkling with mischief.

'Well dear,' said the lady in question, looking a little alarmed. 'I'm a bit old for bumps.'

'How about a cancan?' And without giving her a chance to refuse Cassie tugged Mrs Allingham from the dressing room out on to the stage. She and Emily twined their arms round their elderly friend, and Becky joined on to Emily. Once their line-up was complete, Cassie began humming the famous cancan tune, and the girls went into action, kicking their legs high into the air and giggling helplessly. Mrs Allingham joined in surprisingly vigorously, but was a bit breathless when they eventually laughed themselves to a standstill.

'I haven't enjoyed myself so much for years,' she said, when she had breath to speak. Tears of laughter were spilling down her cheeks.

It was easy to forget, thought Cassie, that only a few minutes before, tears of sadness had been running down theirs for Emily. Now her friend's future was secure, at least for the next year, and Cassie guessed that Mrs Allingham would make sure that her bursary was made available to Emily for as long as she needed it. Perhaps the three friends might manage to stay together at Redwood for the full five years of Lower School? With that hopeful thought, Cassie gave Mrs Allingham, Becky and Emily a last hug and ran off to find her parents.